Fi

and the

Riddle of the Shells

Ellie Mitten

Southernwood Press

Paperback ISBN: 978-1-8380722-2-3
eBook ISBN: 978-1-8380722-3-0

Cover design: Ellie Mitten
Book design: Saltwater Book Design

To Eli and Noa, this story is yours.

xxx

Cornwall

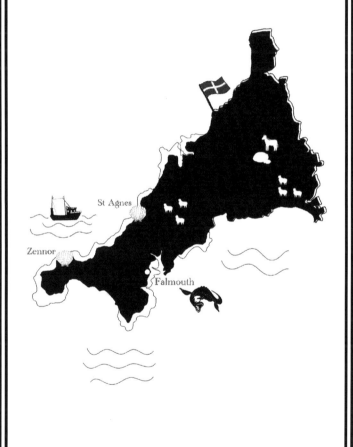

St Agnes

Zennor

Falmouth

One

Trying To Be Normal

It was the summer holidays and Finn longed to be back at school. He was fully aware that this was all wrong, that ten-year-old boys weren't meant to enjoy school and hate the holidays, but there was a lot about Finn that was back to front. He preferred fruit to chocolate, books to footballs, and cartoons were a complete mystery to him. It wasn't these things, however, that made him *really* different.

Sitting on a flowery towel, an island amongst an ocean of sand, Finn watched in confusion as all around him children ran and screamed with delight. If sand got on his book *he* might scream, but it certainly wouldn't be with joy. He hugged his limbs tighter to him, his t-shirt and shorts sticking to his skin thanks to a combination of sweat and a thick layer of sun cream. A pair of socks and sandals prevented any unnecessary sand contact, and a wide-brimmed hat meant he could just about read without squinting, but it was all very uncomfortable.

Beside him, Finn's parents appeared happy enough, but then *they* were human. Unlike Finn. They obviously had the beach loving gene built into them. In a deckchair each, they smiled as they slowly turned pink in the glaring sunshine. His dad even had his t-shirt off, proudly balancing a newspaper on his hairy, round belly. It was an entirely unreasonable sight, in Finn's opinion, but both he and Mum seemed to think it was perfectly normal. As Finn surveyed those around them it was clear they were right. Normal; the description would have made them nothing short of ecstatic. Normal was their dream. In fact, this whole holiday was a not-so-subtle hunt for the normal side of life. Normal in the face of Finn's strangeness.

It had been quite a shock when they'd found that Finn was a wizard, and that was putting it mildly. If Finn remembered correctly, his mum didn't get out of bed for a week. To be fair, it had been pretty surprising. Maybe if there had been some signs as he'd been growing up, any strange happenings that could have given them a clue, but no. He'd been entirely ordinary. Entirely *human*. No unexplained events at all. Therefore, when a knock at the door had interrupted his seventh birthday, and two bespectacled individuals had stood on the doorstep claiming to have important news about Finn and his future, they'd all thought it was an elaborate joke. His dad even searched the sitting room for hidden cameras. Mr Smalls and Mrs Turnpike weren't a hoax, however. They'd come to inform them about Finn's magic, and how it would develop now he was seven. Stunned, open-mouthed silence had followed the declaration, but their disbelief was short lived. It had been hard to deny magic was real after Mrs Turnpike had turned the sofa into an elephant, and Mr Smalls had produced a chocolate cake out of thin air. At that point, Finn was sold. He didn't care how magic existed. He didn't care if he'd have to give anything up. He wanted to be a wizard more than he'd ever wanted anything. The thought that, one day, he'd be able to perform such feats was too tantalising to resist. Mum and Dad, though, were not so easily won over. Hours of questions followed. They asked for all sorts of boring information, like how they *knew* Finn was a wizard.

Apparently, it was very rare for a wizard to be born into a human family, and had something to do with being the first born of a second born of a third born and so on and so on. Finn didn't really take it all in. It was a bit much for a 7-year-old's attention span when there was a floating cake in the room. Whatever the reason, Mum and Dad didn't appreciate being so special. Despite over three years having passed, they were still struggling with the change to their lives. To their credit, though, they hadn't stood in Finn's way. They didn't try to stop him embracing his new future, or from starting a new school so he could learn to wield his magic. Even when it was revealed he'd have to stay during the week, only returning home for weekends and holidays, they'd swallowed their own misgivings and nodded. Their only condition was to remain ignorant. They could accept that magic was real but they'd rather not know any more, thank you very much! The fact they let him go at all told Finn how much they loved him. It was the main reason he tried so hard to be what they wanted during their time together. Or, at least, tried to try. It wasn't easy.

"Fancy a dip?" called Dad, interrupting Finn's thoughts.

Finn frowned, bemused for a second. This was their first day in the unreasonably sunny seaside town of Falmouth, and he'd yet to understand all the weird things that were expected of him. He squinted up from beneath his fringe of brownish, blonde hair, shaking it to one side to check Dad wasn't teasing him.

"A swim? What, in the sea?" he asked, horrified.

He'd noticed all the bodies gleefully throwing themselves into the waves but had vaguely wondered if it was some sort of bet. Or a sponsored event for charity.

"Of course the sea," laughed Dad. "It'll be ever so refreshing."

Finn frowned at him as if he'd lost his mind, realising there were limits to the lengths he'd go for the sake of his parents. Jumping into the ocean, the literal home of sharks, was definitely beyond those limits.

"Oo, I'll come with you," said Mum, putting down her book and lifting her sunglasses onto her head. "It looks beautiful."

Finn looked from her to the expanse of blue in complete confusion. He supposed the glistening surface was pretty but it was also vast. He could easily imagine all the man-eating creatures that would fit in it. The fact no man-eating fish inhabited the waters around Cornwall was irrelevant to Finn, as it was not one that he knew. As clever as he was about all things magical, the human world generally baffled him.

"Come on Finn, you'll love it," encouraged Mum.

Finn bit back the rude retort that had been forming on his lips. "Hmm, maybe in a minute," he said instead, waving his book in the air. "I'm enjoying reading my book whilst trying not to melt at the moment."

He tried to keep the sarcasm out of his voice, he really did, but from the pinched expression on Mum's face he knew he'd failed.

"Keep the cover on that thing," warned Dad sternly before they both walked away.

Finn looked at the book he was still holding aloft. It was one of a small selection he'd been allowed to bring, but not before he'd swapped the covers with more "acceptable" titles. This one was brightly coloured, boasting to contain an amusing story about football. In reality, it housed a compendium of spells Finn was attempting to learn. Or learn as best he could without his wand. Every time he left school, whether for the entire summer or a single night, they would confiscate his wand and bind his magic. It was borderline torture. Everyone else was trusted, as they had wizard parents to keep them in line, but the possibility of Finn "alerting the humans to the existence of wizards" was too risky, or so he'd been told when he'd started school. Every year he'd argue that he was older, more trustworthy, blah blah blah, but his head teacher wouldn't budge. So here he was magic-less, which, in his opinion, was the worst possible thing to be.

It was teatime before Finn's parents finally conceded that they'd been at the beach long enough. The cottage they were renting was only across the road, so it wasn't a long walk back, but Finn still winced at every step as sand rubbed him in all sorts of unmentionable places. After they'd eaten, Mum and Dad pulled out stacks of maps and guidebooks, spreading them out on the table.

"Come and look, Finn," they called. "We can start planning our itinerary for the week."

Finn grimaced.

"This looks fun," cried Mum, picking up a leaflet with a boat on the front. The boat was full of people, all grinning idiotically as they careered, presumably at high speed, through the water. "It says here that you can rent boats of all shapes and sizes from the harbour. That's definitely one for the list. Maybe tomorrow?"

Dad was nodding enthusiastically as he made notes.

"I'll pencil it in," he said, drawing a mini timetable on a blank piece of paper.

"Nothing like organised fun," commented Finn dryly.

7

"Come on, Finn," encouraged Dad. "Have a look through some of these, see what you fancy?"

He threw a pile of brochures at Finn before returning to his timetable.

It was only ten days, Finn told himself. He could cope for ten days.

All his conviction vanished the next morning as he stood on a harbour wall wearing a bright orange life jacket. The boat they'd rented for the day was tied up next to them, and Mum and Dad were filling it with food, blankets, fishing equipment and goodness knows what else. The little vessel seemed undeterred by the added weight as it bobbed merrily.

As Finn climbed aboard, movement rolled through him.

"Does that stop?" he asked. "Once we get moving?"

The man untying the rope laughed.

"City kids," he muttered to himself, before pushing them off unceremoniously, not bothering to watch as they lurched forward. Finn gripped the edge for dear life. They drifted gently, bobbing haphazardly with no real purpose until Dad managed to pull the engine cord hard enough to get the motor started.

"Left is right and right is left," Mum called over the noise as Dad pushed the rudder from side to side.

The boat did a full 360-degree turn before Dad got it heading straight, and roughly in the desired direction.

"I think I might be sick," mumbled Finn, and he huddled up near the front, wrapping himself in a blanket.

"Isn't this fun?" Mum called to him.

He smiled feebly in response before turning and focusing on where they were going. Dad didn't seem to be the best sailor, and Finn wanted some forewarning if they were about to crash into another boat. Drowning *wasn't* top on his to do list.

As it happened, Finn didn't hate life on a boat as much as he thought he would. Once he'd got used to the disconcerting rocking, it was actually quite peaceful. He wasn't a massive fan of large groups of people, human or wizard, so being protected from potential social encounters by vast swathes of water suited him nicely. Until, that is, Mum and Dad decided that reading his book wasn't "fun" enough, and he should really give fishing a go.

"Why?" he grumbled.

"You might enjoy it," answered Dad.

"Yes, but there's also the overwhelming possibility that I won't."

Dad frowned at him, and Finn knew he'd said the

wrong thing again. He sighed but tucked his fringe behind one ear and took the proffered bag with a plastic crabbing set inside. He knew the origin of this idea only too well; he'd seen the guilty book in a bag when they'd first arrived. *1001 Activities for Boys* was a small volume but, when Finn had peeked inside, full of things like fishing. A disturbing number had also involved sticks, and not the wand kind. Human boys were definitely weird.

"You'll need this too," said Mum, holding out a second bag.

"What is it?" he asked, squeezing the silvery contents through the sealed plastic.

"Bait."

"Huh?"

"Dead fish. It's what you use as bait."

Finn blanched in horror.

"You capture fish, using fish?" he asked. "Why don't we just stick with the fish we already have rather than throwing it in the sea? Much less hassle, surely?"

Dad laughed, but Finn really hadn't been joking.

"You'll catch much bigger fish than those if you're lucky."

Finn peered at the specimens he held. They were certainly small, but he wasn't sure about catching something *much* bigger. What if the thing he caught decided his fingers were a tastier bait?

"Come on," encouraged Dad. "I'll set it up for you."

Luckily for Finn, he proved to be a terrible fisherman. Every time he pulled in his line, all that hung off the hook were stands of seaweed and an increasingly nibbled piece of bait. The lack of action also meant he could sneakily read at the same time.

"Look at that shoal," cried Mum. "Check your line Finn, there were hundreds of them."

Muttering, but not loudly enough for them to hear, Finn did as he was told.

"Oh no, just more seaweed," moaned Mum, peering over his shoulder. "I thought we'd have a dozen mackerel for dinner by now. Maybe stick another piece of bait on?"

Finn wrinkled his nose as he dutifully pulled out another tiny fish. They might be small in size, but they made up for it in stink factor.

"Maybe mackerel just have a decent sense of smell and swim in the opposite direction at the first whiff?" he grumbled, but Mum wasn't listening.

Finn held the offending object as far from him as he could, right over the side of the boat, as he pushed the hook through the fish's cold flesh. He shuddered at the sensation, and his hand slipped.

"Ow!" he cried.

The sharp end of metal had gone right through the fish bait and into his finger. Blood swelled, and he clenched his fist in pain. Droplets of red ran down his hand and into the water.

"Stupid fishing," Finn mumbled to himself as he wiped blood on the blanket wrapped around his legs.

His eyes wandered to where he'd dropped the hook in shock. The thin line of plastic twine was just visible beneath the surface, before the murkiness of the sea swallowed it from sight. As he watched, a shadow loomed, approaching too quickly to be a mass of seaweed. It grew and grew, getting closer every second, until the whole expanse in front of the boat had gone dark. Finn sat upright in alarm and was about to call to Mum and Dad when the line yanked tight. The plastic handle that lay at his feet was pulled forward and, acting on instinct, Finn stamped his foot down on it to stop it from flying overboard. The cord went tense, the boat rocking dramatically for one second. Then, in an instance, all was still. The shadow had gone, and the line fell slack. Rattled, Finn pulled it in, but only a few inches came out. The rest was gone; hook, bait and all.

Two

Men-an-Tol

After that, Finn was less keen than before to enter the water.

"Do they have sharks off the coast here?" he asked Mum and Dad. "Or whales?"

They laughed.

"Seals," said Mum. "Quite a few. Apparently, there's one down at St. Ives that likes to take the odd nip out of the local surfers."

"I think basking sharks have been seen in places, too," Dad added knowledgeably, "but they're gentle giants. Nothing to worry about."

"Hmm," mused Finn. He hadn't told them about the shadow, but he couldn't get it out of his mind.

"Maybe we should try somewhere inland tomorrow?" he suggested that evening, as the guidebooks came out again. He'd decided he should probably take a more active role in planning their outings. That way, he could steer things in the least awful direction. And hopefully avoid ending up in the middle of the sea again.

"Ok," said Mum, delighted he was getting involved. "You pick. Anything you want."

She looked at him with such enthusiastic happiness that Finn couldn't bring himself to admit he just wanted to go home. Instead, he reached out and grabbed the brochure closest to him.

"Look," he said, glancing at the one he'd picked, "a stone with a hole in the middle. That should be fascinating."

"Men-an-Tol," read Dad, flicking to the relevant section of the guidebook he held. "It says here that it's an ancient stone from the Bronze Age era. It's believed to hold fertility properties. For centuries, women have climbed through it to help them get pregnant."

Mum laughed.

"And," went on Dad, pausing uncertainly, "it…," he gulped, "it's meant to be guarded by a piskie that grants cures or special gifts to those it chooses."

There was an awkward pause. This was the sort of "magic stuff" that Mum and Dad liked to avoid at all costs. That it was merely some old story didn't matter. Since discovering magic and wizards were real, a question mark had been placed over many aspects of life. As they refused to talk about it, or ask Finn what was true, it only made the possibilities more vast and threatening.

The silence grew for a moment before Mum managed a big, strained smile.

"We can take a picnic," she declared.

If Finn was someone who believed in bad omens, he might have worried that they got lost no less than five times before they finally pulled into the tiny car park that was little more than a pull-in off the road. To his amazement, it was full, and they had to wait for a space to become available. As he sat, Finn stared absentmindedly out of the window. A collection of families were gathered around their vehicles, unloading chairs and what looked like the biggest picnic ever. Masses of children were being loaded up and pushed in the direction of the rough, moorland grass that stretched away from the layby. Blankets awaited their armfuls but, once dumped, the children all ran off, chasing each other and laughing. A small lump appeared in Finn's throat as the sight brought back memories. Memories of a life before his dramatic seventh birthday. Back when he'd had friends. They'd played together endlessly, the game itself changing over the years, but the fun remaining the same. When he'd started at St. Humphries, however, things changed. He was out of the loop. Left behind. He couldn't share what he'd been up to, no matter how cool, and compared to real magic their games felt boring. As the months passed, the invites to play dates stopped coming. At first, Finn had been too wrapped up in his new life to notice. By the time the loneliness started to bite, it was too late. St. Humphries offered no replacements either. After the initial interest in *The Human*, Finn's non-magical upbringing set him too firmly apart. To say he had no friends would be extreme. There were a few others who'd chat to him throughout the day, but it wasn't true friendship. They were more companions of convenience. A bunch of fellow outsiders that hung out together because no other options were available to them. Not like the friends Finn read about in books. Most of the time he didn't mind and preferred to spend his time studying. Even as magic became his norm, it never stopped being… well, magical. The way a simple combination of words could conjure objects out of nothing. Or how mixing the most mundane collection of ingredients could create a substance that would make him invisible. The human world had nothing to compete with that.

Finn dragged his attention away from the playing children and opened his book.

It wasn't much longer until a space became available, and Dad steered the car into it, turning off the engine at last. The air was refreshing when Finn got out, but he kept his head down, refusing to look at the children still running about as he ploughed his way up the hill to where they would find the stones. He wasn't sure what he was expecting, but from the sheer number of visitors, it was more than what greeted him. Three stones stood, in a wonky line, jutting upwards. Two of them would have been totally insignificant if they hadn't bracketed the third; a stone hoop, jauntily emerging from the earth. It was cool in a way, Finn supposed, but still. They'd been driving for over an hour to get here. Bemused, he looked around again, but no. There was nothing else. Apparently, he was the only one unimpressed. People were milling about everywhere, delighted grins on their faces as they waited for their turn to approach the central stone. There was practically a queue. One by one they posed for photographs, each poking their head hilariously through the middle of the circular stone.

"Are all these people seriously here to look at a stone version of a hula hoop?" he asked, unable to contain his confusion any further.

"Come on Finn," called Mum, beckoning him over and not listening to his musings. "Pop your head through. I'll get a photo."

"Why don't you do it?" he asked, having no desire to look stupid.

"I don't want another baby," she laughed. She was joking, but there was a slight edge to her voice, as if she feared the legend might be true. Finn had certainly heard of weirder things in some of his classes, but he didn't believe for one second that this old lump of rock held any magical properties. That was just nonsense.

Sighing, Finn dutifully approached the stone and poked his head through the centre, trying his best to force his freckled face to smile and not grimace at the camera.

"Lovely," called Mum.

"Now crawl through." Dad called.

Finn frowned.

"It'll be fun," Dad went on before Finn could refuse.

Finn refrained from asking why, if it was all so "fun", it wasn't *Dad* on his hands and knees in the mud, but he shot him a glare that conveyed his displeasure.

"Humans are mad," he muttered to himself as he started to crawl, attempting to avoid scraping his bare kneecaps on the rough stone. "I wish this holiday wasn't so dull."

A sharp pain lanced through his hand as he placed it on the earth.

"Ouch," he cried, lifting it back up quickly. He couldn't see what had cut him, but the earth was rough with stones and thistles. When he looked at his hand, he saw two identical puncture wounds, blood blooming from them.

"Another injury," joked Dad, helping Finn to his feet. "Careful, or your hands will be covered in plasters by the end of the week."

He gestured to Finn's other hand, where a beige plaster covered the cut from the fishing hook. The sight bothered Finn more than it should. As a wizard, he could heal cuts in seconds when he had his magic. If any of his classmates saw him with a plaster, he'd never hear the end of it.

For a moment, the separation from his magic was too much. Tears welled, glistening in the midday sun.

"Oh Finn, does it hurt that badly?" asked Mum, stroking his cheek and pulling him in for a hug.

Finn opened his mouth to say it wasn't the cut, but he closed it again almost instantly. He couldn't explain, not to them, not when it was the lack of magic that caused him pain. Initially, when they'd insisted on knowing nothing about Finn's new life, he hadn't cared, but the older he got the sadder it made him. Magic was everything to him. And he was good at it too, one of the best in his entire class, despite his heritage. But he couldn't share any of it with them. Couldn't make them proud. Couldn't tell them that magic was now so entwined with his identity that he wasn't sure who he was during these times he was forced to be without it.

Briskly, he wiped his eyes on the back of his wrist.

"I'm fine," he said firmly. "Can we have the picnic now?"

He'd had his fill of the stones. It seemed, whether or not he involved himself in the decision making, the results were the same; boredom and bleeding fingers. He may as well leave it up to Mum and Dad from now on. At least then he could blame them when it all went wrong.

Three

Monsters At Midnight

As Mum tucked Finn into bed that night, she opened his window, pulling the thin curtains to block out the moon.

"It's going to be a warm night," she said before kissing him on the head. "Night darling."

"Night," Finn replied, settling down. Their cottage wasn't far from the beach, and the sound of the sea swam in through the open window. It wasn't an unpleasant noise, however, and Finn quickly drifted off to sleep, the salty air a refreshing change from London pollution.

As evening slipped smoothly into night, Finn slept on. The moon lit up the sky and the stars came out, reflecting onto the water. A humming started drifting through the air, out of the sea and up, up into Finn's bedroom. The melody caressed him awake, or at least he opened his eyes and swung his legs out of bed, but he wasn't conscious. If anyone saw him, they'd probably assume he was sleepwalking, but he wasn't. The enchantment that pulled at him could not be so simply explained.

Mum and Dad were fast asleep, unaware as Finn turned the key in the lock and let himself out of the front door. The air was cool against his exposed arms, but Finn didn't notice. His bare feet moved him forwards, across the thankfully empty road and down the slope to the beach. The tide was out, and he walked down the wet sand all the way to the water's edge. When it lapped at his toes he stopped, frozen in place. The hum from the sea continued and he swayed slightly where he stood, staring without seeing. If he had been able to see, he certainly wouldn't have remained so calmly in place. Before him, out of the waves, a dark shape emerged. It's head, when it first rose, might have been mistaken for a seal's, if it hadn't been for the wicked horns that protruded from beside its ears. Its skin was black and sleek. Nostrils flat. Its eyes glistening dark spheres. As the creature rose higher, its true size was revealed. Its neck was thick and long with jagged spikes running down its spine.

The main bulk of its body remained beneath the water, strong flippers propelling it forward until it rested directly in front of Finn. It opened its mouth to reveal rows of sharp, white teeth that glinted in the moonlight.

Still, Finn did not move. As the monster lowered its head, an almighty cry pierced the air. The beast stopped in its tracks as a tiny figure ran forwards, brandishing a pickaxe before him. It careered towards the pair, and the humming halted.

Finn blinked once, then glanced up. He screamed in fear at the sight that met him, stumbling backwards even as the pickaxe wielding figure leapt past him and waved his weapon in the creature's face.

"Get back," it cried fiercely, his accent as thick and Cornish as any Finn had heard on their trip so far.

As Finn continued to scramble up the beach, he watched in amazement as the beast retreated. Seconds later, it was gone, leaving not even a ripple in its wake. Finn lay on the sand, reeling, his body his own again but strangely numb with shock. He simply stared and stared at the now empty space where the *thing* had loomed. Was he dreaming? Or had he actually just escaped the jaws of a vicious sea monster?

"Well, that was close," a voice piped up, drawing Finn's attention away from the sea and to the face of a... But Finn's brain didn't have the word to describe what had spoken. It was human in form, but so small that it obviously wasn't. Standing at no more than two-feet-high, it shared many of the characteristics of a ceramic garden gnome. His head appeared overly large, and was covered with an impressively thick beard. In fact, hair seemed to grow from more places than just his chin. His large, bulbous nose and elf-like pointy ears also boasted their own hairy forests, each sprouting erratically. A wrinkled face smiled at him from under a hard hat fixed with a torch that shone in the darkness. His clothes were simple but ripped all over and covered in dirt. He held a pickaxe in his hand, which he used to gesticulate with when he talked.

Finn shrank back even more.

"Are you alright?" he was saying, peering at Finn from under his bushy eyebrows. "That was all a bit dramatic, wasn't it?"

"Who… what… who…" Finn stammered, but his brain and mouth weren't communicating properly enough to form actual sentences.

"I'd been planning a much more civilized first meeting," the thing went on, apparently unaware of Finn's mini break down, "preferably over breakfast. Or lunch. Lunch is my favourite, although dinner's pretty good too. Or brunch. Or tea. Anything with food really."

As the chatter washed over him, Finn calmed his breathing enough to speak.

"Wh- what was that?" he asked. "Wh -what just happened?"

"What, with the morgawr?" said the little man, pausing his list of acceptable mealtimes. "Crazy, wasn't it? I've never seen a morgawr behave like that before. They're usually quite friendly, in their own way."

"Yeah," scoffed Finn, "it was a right charmer. Positively delightful. I feel bad now for not saying hello, but I was a bit distracted by it trying to bite my head off." Words spewed from his mouth as indignation took over from shock.

"Actually," corrected the… thing, "I believe, in the rare cases a morgawr goes for anything bigger than a fish, they like to drown their prey. I imagine he was trying to drag you into the water, not bite your head off."

Finn's eyes widened in horror. This couldn't be real. A dream was far more likely, he told himself. Releasing a breath, he decided to go with it. There was no point in getting worried about a dream, however unusual.

"Who are you?" he asked.

"Oh, I'm sorry, I forgot my manners in all the confusion. I'm Norman." He gave a bow. "But you can call me Norm."

"And… and…" Finn struggled to find a polite way to phrase his next question, but failed. "*What* are you?"

"I'm a Knocker," Norm replied, in a way that suggested Finn would know what the hell that was.

"A… what?"

"A Knocker," Norm repeated. "A *Cornish* Knocker."

"Err…"

Norm frowned and then, inexplicably, sniffed at Finn.

"What are you doing?" asked Finn, backing up slightly.

"Smelling your blood."

"Well, that's creepy."

"I'm just checking you're the right one. And you are."

"The right *what*?"

"The one with magical blood that I claimed earlier," explained Norm. "And it's definitely you. You *do* know you're a wizard, don't you?"

"Of course I know I'm a wizard," replied Finn, deeply freaked out by Norm's knowledge on the subject. "But what do you mean, the one you *claimed*?"

Norm ignored the question.

"So, you know you're a wizard, but you've never heard of a Cornish Knocker?"

"Should I have?" Finn asked.

"Well, I know we're not the most glamourous of magical

creatures, but I didn't know we'd slipped off the radar entirely. What about the morgawr? I bet they teach you all about sea dragons?"

"Err, no," admitted Finn. "I haven't learnt much about any magical creatures. I don't think we touch on them much at school. Maybe next year?"

"But what about at home?" asked Norm incredulously. "Bedtime stories?"

"My parents are human," explained Finn. "We have bedtime stories about Gruffalos and the three little pigs."

Norm's eyebrows rose so high they disappeared beneath his hat. "How odd. Well, at least I can be less insulted that you've never heard of me."

"So, err, what are you?" Finn asked again. "I mean, what is a Cornish Knocker? I'm guessing from the name you only live in Cornwall?"

"The Cornish variety do, of course, but we have relations in other areas too. Wales and," he curled his lip slightly and wrinkled his nose before adding, in a disgusted tone, "*Devon*."

"I've never been to either of those places," said Finn.

"I guess that further excuses your ignorance."

Finn tried not to grit his teeth at the repeated insult.

"Anyway, we're all mine dwellers," Norm went on. "Sort

of like a dwarf, but without the temper, or a piskie, without the magic."

"What do you do down the mines?" asked Finn, skating over the mention of other magical creatures he knew nothing about.

"That depends. Some of us can cause a bit of mischief. Lead the miners down the wrong path, steal their pasties, that sort of thing. Most of us are helpful, though, watching out for the miners. Warning them if a cave is about to collapse."

"So... so you're good?"

"Of course! I mean, I've had the odd evil cousin that liked to lure miners to their deaths, but we don't talk about them."

"I'm not surprised!" exclaimed Finn.

"You don't need to worry about me, though," Norm went on as if Finn hadn't commented, "I'm here to serve. You've been claimed by one of the best!"

"Hang on. You said that before too. What do you mean, "claimed" me? I'm a person. You can't claim me."

"I can. I bit you. Earlier, at the standing stone. And I'm definitely the first, I could taste it in your blood."

Finn grimaced. "That was you? When I cut my hand? Not a sharp stone? You bit me?"

"Sorry," said Norm looking bashful. "I didn't mean for it to hurt. And it's the only way I could think of to grant your wish."

"What?" asked Finn.

"At the stone."

As Norm spoke, a memory came back to Finn. A memory of himself muttering in anger about how he wished this holiday was less dull. He gasped.

"I thought that stone made you pregnant, not granted wishes?" he cried.

"Well, the two theories got a bit mixed over the years. Most people wished for a baby, so it's what they started to believe was the main purpose of the stone. The piskie who lives there will grant any wish she deems worthy, however."

Finn dropped his head into his hands. "I wasn't making a wish," he insisted. "I was grumbling. I take it back. I wish for this holiday to be as boring as before. No sea dragons, no knockers, none of it!"

"I'm sorry, but none of this," Norm held out his arms and gestured to the sea and where Finn lay in the sand, "is a wish. The piskie is on holiday, that's why I was there. She asked me to watch the place, keep note of any wishes that she might need to know about, but I don't possess any magic. The only way I could help was by claiming you. So, I'm not responsible for the morgawr, or whatever enchantment you were under. Only me." Norm's face fell with sadness. "I thought you'd be pleased."

Finn closed his eyes. His brain couldn't cope. He was used to the bizarre being real, but this was too much.

It's only a dream, he reminded himself. Or maybe he'd fallen out of bed and hit his head, and this was some wild hallucination? He pinched his arm, nails digging deeply until pain forced him to stop. When he opened his eyes, he was still sitting on the wet sand and the knocker was staring at him with a puzzled expression on his face.

"Are you alright?" he asked. "You look a bit pale."

"I'm going back to the cottage," said Finn. Maybe if he went to bed, Norm would have vanished by the time he woke up?

"I'll come with you."

"No!" cried Finn. "No, thank you. I'm fine."

"But… I'm yours now." Norm had such a dejected look on his face Finn didn't know what to do.

This was madness, but...

"Fine," he sighed. "Come. For now."

Norm's face split into a grin as Finn pushed himself to his feet and brushed the sand off his pyjamas as best as he could. Sand in his bed was going to raise questions from Mum and Dad. Questions they wouldn't like the answers to.

"Oh, you dropped your bottle by the way," said Norm as Finn turned to leave.

Frowning, Finn looked at the green bottle the knocker was holding out to him. It was sealed with a cork and there was something inside.

"It's not mine," he said, although he took it anyway. Refusing seemed too much effort. "Let's go," he said.

The walk back to the cottage took forever. Finn's bare feet hurt with every step, and cold was seeping into his bones. He carried the bottle in one hand, and the tiny knocker bounded along happily beside him. Despite Finn's frequent shushes, Norm appeared unable *not* to talk. Mostly it was nonsense, a running commentary on their journey.

The stress of being discovered did nothing to appease the increasing pressure inside Finn's head. Thankfully, once outside the cottage, his demands for quiet were finally taken seriously. He barely breathed as he tiptoed through the house and up to his room, letting out a massive sigh when he found himself safely behind his bedroom door. His heart pounded way too fast in his chest.

"This is nice," said Norm.

Finn glanced up to see the knocker bounding jovially on his bed.

"Stop it," he hissed. "You have to be quiet!"

"Oh, ok," said Norm, in an overly loud whisper. "Why?"

"My parents are asleep, and if they wake up, they'll…" Finn hesitated. He didn't know what exactly they'd do, but fainting was probably high on the list. That would be before the screaming and shouting began. Clearly inhuman, miniature bearded men covered in coal dust definitely went against every agreement to pretend the magical world wasn't real. Finn ran his free hand through his hair, despairingly, at which point he realised he was still carrying the bottle from the beach. Holding it up to the moonlight streaming in his bedroom window, he saw that it contained a rolled-up piece of paper. Deciding he couldn't cope with any more weirdness, he placed it firmly on his chest of drawers before turning back to Norm.

"Aren't you going to see what it is?" enquired Norm.

"No," replied Finn firmly. "Tomorrow I'll throw it right back in the sea."

Norm raised an eyebrow in surprise, but Finn continued to talk, more to himself than anyone else.

"Actually, I won't have to," he muttered, "because none

of this is real!" He let out a slightly crazed laugh. "Tomorrow, I'll wake up nice and refreshed, and all this will be a distant memory. A bad dream. In fact, I'm putting an end to this right now."

With that, he strode over to his bed, pulled back the covers and determinedly snuggled down. He pretended not to notice when he felt the weight of the knocker climb up and settle down beside him. He merely pulled the covers more tightly over himself and muttered,

"It's a dream. Just a dream. Everything will be ok in the morning."

Four

It Wasn't A Dream

When the sun rose the next morning, piercing through the curtains, Finn let out a groan. His skull felt like it was full of cotton wool. He rolled over, away from the light, and buried his face in his pillow. Images danced around his head, remnants from the strangest dream. He stretched his legs out under the duvet, then froze as his skin brushed over something scratchy. Sand? Impossible. His sheets had been perfectly clean when Mum had tucked him in the evening before. Warily, he opened his eyes, only just managing to contain his scream. Spread out on his pillow, dribbling freely, was… was…. *the knocker!*

Finn squeezed his eyes shut again. He was hallucinating, surely? Or maybe he was still asleep? Slowly, he cracked one eye open again, enough to make out the snoring figure, before slamming it shut again.

No. No, no, no, he chanted to himself. This could not be real. Because if the knocker was real, then that meant the terrifying, stomach curdling Morgawr from his dream was real too. And Finn simply couldn't accept that.

Please be a dream, please be a dream, he muttered under his breath.

The fart the knocker let out in response was not the answer Finn had been hoping for. Gagging at the smell, he threw himself backwards, falling to the floor with a crash.

Amazingly, neither the loud thump of his body hitting the floor nor his cry of pain did anything to wake up… *Norm.* The name popped into Finn's mind as the details of the night before came back to him, in unwelcome detail.

"I can eat him for you, if you want?"

Startled, Finn spun around to find a cat sitting on his windowsill. There was no sign of who had spoken, however, and Finn glanced back to check if it had been him.

"I doubt he'll taste very nice, but if it'd help, I'm willing to do it. You'd have to remove the axe first, though, that would just get stuck in my throat."

Finn wheeled back in time to see the cat's mouth moving in time with the words. Despite what his eyes were telling him, Finn continued to look around. His brain refused to believe that a cat was talking to him. It just wasn't possible.

"Are you quite alright?" the cat enquired, peering forward.

Finn opened and closed his mouth repeatedly, rather like a fish, but no response came out. What could he say?

No, because I've gone mad and my head is about to explode, sounded rather dramatic, even under the current circumstances. Instead, he stared. The newcomer was rather large for a cat, with sleek fur patterned with brown stripes that ranged from a dark beige to a deep chocolate. His eyes glowed yellow, unnervingly intelligent. Even without speech, he clearly wasn't 'normal'.

Just then the knocker woke up with an elaborate yawn.

"Oh bother Tomkin, what are you doing 'ere?" he asked the cat, apparently more annoyed than surprised to see him.

"Same as you, I imagine, old friend."

"Ah, but you're too late. He's mine. I claimed him."

The knocker puffed out his chest proudly. The new day had done little to alter his strangeness. He'd taken off his hard hat, and his hair grew in tangled tufts, almost as wild as his beard. His gnarled face and large, pointed ears were so obviously not human it took Finn's breath away.

The cat, though, looked distinctly unimpressed.

"An old-fashioned rule," he scorned. "They can have more than one of us, in my opinion."

"Your opinion? You think *your* opinion overrides centuries of tradition? And how'd you even know he was 'ere?"

If it was possible for a cat to shrug, then that was exactly what it did. Disregarding the knocker's snort of annoyance, it turned to Finn instead.

"May I present myself formally; I am Tomkin, although you may know me by my 'human' title. They seem to have bestowed the moniker of *The Beast of Bodmin Moor* upon me. All a tad dramatic…"

"Which you love!" interrupted Norm.

Tomkin ignored him again, apparently waiting for Finn to show some sign of impressed recognition at the name.

"You're… you're… you're a talking cat," Finn stammered instead.

Norm let out a delighted snort.

Tomkin rolled his eyes.

"Are you unfamiliar with my legend?"

"Um…"

The cat glared at Finn. "Legend tells," he said in a

mysterious voice, "that a giant, ferocious feline roams the moorland around Bodmin. It lives in the shadows, impossible to catch, as elusive as smoke. It terrorises the local livestock, tearing out the throats of sheep before devouring their flesh."

Finn's eyes grew wide.

"And do you?" he asked, wrinkling his nose in disgust.

"Well… no," admitted Tomkin after a pause. "Do you have any idea how messy it is gnawing through wool?" He shuddered, and Finn noticed his fur gleamed impeccably in the morning sun. "Such hard work too. No, no, it's much easier to sneak into people's houses and steal from their fridges."

"Oh, ok," said Finn, somewhat relieved. "But is that seriously you?"

"Why do you doubt it?" enquired Tomkin.

Finn considered his answer, not wanting to appear rude. "It's just… you're not that big."

"Ah, but people see what they want to see," replied Tomkin, as if that explained everything.

"Can all cats talk?" asked Finn. He had a cat at home. It never seemed to like him, but the thought it was *ignoring* him, after he'd let it sleep on his bed, made Finn quite indignant.

"No," scoffed Tomkin. "I'm from a long line of magical

cats. *Cat Siths* are what you'd call my ancestors."

"Cat Siths? As in, the fairy cats?" Finn's disbelief was clear in his tone. "You can't be serious? They're extinct! No one's reported a sighting in half a century. Not in this country, anyway."

"Maybe they've all been looking in the wrong places," said Tomkin mysteriously.

"This is ridiculous," cried Finn. Then, to himself, "Maybe I'm going mad? Yes, that would make sense."

Tomkin and Norm exchanged a look.

"He's a bit clueless about… *our* kind," explained Norm in an overly loud whisper. "They don't teach them about magical creatures in school these days, apparently."

"They don't… what?" spluttered Tomkin. "I've always known wizards were arrogant, but not to pass on the knowledge of *my* kind? I ask you! What do you learn then, boy?"

"Magic!" exclaimed Finn in frustration. "They teach me magic, and I happen to be rather good at it. Maybe there's just not time for… stories?!"

"Stories are everything," growled Tomkin. "Myths aren't just stories, they're truth hidden in plain sight. Many may have forgotten about us, but we're still here. My existence is all the truth you need, surely?"

Finn sighed, but couldn't refute the cat's logic.

"Ok, ok, if I'm not going mad, which I still think is highly possible, then I accept that at least *some* of what you're saying must be true. But if that's the case, why don't I know about it?"

Tomkin snorted.

"We're beneath the interest of most wizards," he said. "They're happy to let us become legends for children. We're all fading from the world. They probably can't be bothered with things that won't be around for much longer."

"That's sad. Why are you fading?"

"Our homes are being destroyed by humans at every turn. There are a few spots where we cling on tighter. Places with fewer people, like Cornwall. We won't be able to hold out forever, though."

"As fascinating and informative as this all is, Tomkin," Norm said before Finn could enquire further, "you didn't answer my earlier question; how did you know he was here?"

"My sense of smell might not be as good as it used to be, but I can smell unclaimed magical blood from miles away."

"Humph. Well, it's not unclaimed anymore."

"Do you think that'll stop any others if they get a whiff of him? What if something less friendly than me comes along? You might want to think about asking me to stay."

"I'm not exactly defenceless," said Norm, tapping his axe.

"You're not a 'beast', though, are you?"

Norm sniffed and was about to argue further when Finn interrupted.

"As this is my house, well, my holiday house, then I think *I* get to decide who's allowed to stay."

Both creatures paused and looked at him as if they'd forgotten he was even in the room.

"Maybe I don't want either of you," Finn powered on.

"But… but…" Norm stammered. "I *claimed* you."

Finn clenched his teeth together as he turned away from the pair of them. His head ached, and he was struggling to think clearly. Through the wall he could hear his parents stirring, another complication. He paced, his mind whirring, and then his gaze fell on the tiny bottle he'd carried back from the beach the night before. It appeared to glow. To distract himself from the turmoil of his thoughts, he picked it up. Not fully aware of what he was doing, he unstopped the cork and pulled out a curled-up piece of parchment. Unfurling it, he read, a deep frown appearing on his brow.

He read through the words again. Then a third time, nevertheless, it made no sense. With a grunt of annoyance, he slammed the bottle back on the side. Of course, nothing could be simple that morning.

"What does it say?" piped up Norm, watching Finn from the bed.

"I don't know," said Finn. "I don't understand a word."

"Oh, can't you read?" asked Norm sympathetically. "That explains a lot." He gave Tomkin a sideways glance.

"No!" replied Finn crossly. "Of course I can read. It's the *words* that are little more than nonsense."

He flung the paper at Norm to prove his point.

Squinting, and holding the paper at an absurdly close to his nose, Norm read. Tomkin, too, leapt onto the bed and peered at the slanted writing.

"It makes perfect sense to me," Norm announced after a moment.

Tomkin nodded before padding the duvet and circling on the spot.

"What!" cried Finn indignantly. "What does it mean then?"

"It's a plea for help from someone who calls themselves a *Sea Princess*," answered Norm, holding the note back out to Finn. "Of course, there are no such things as sea princesses. Much more likely that it's a mermaid, or sea witch, with notions of grandeur."

"Well, I don't care anyway," said Finn, re-rolling the

message and pushing it firmly back into the bottle. "I'm going to throw it back into the sea the first opportunity I get."

"You can't do that!" gasped Norm. "Just because she over inflated her title don't mean you can ignore her."

Finn took a deep breath. It was all too much. He closed his eyes, willing the world to return to normal. When he opened them again, however, it hadn't.

"I need breakfast," he announced.

"Oo, goody," cried Norm, the bottle and its message apparently entirely forgotten. "I'm starving! One thing you'll have to learn about knockers, is that they're always hungry. And I mean *always*!"

"You can't come! My parents are human. They'll…" Finn trailed off. He didn't want to think what Mum and Dad would do if they saw Norm. "You must not leave this room," he instructed instead.

"Oh, you don't need to worry about that. Humans can't see or hear magical creatures, not unless they really need to."

"I don't care," said Finn, not sure if he fully believed Norm or not. "I need to think, and I don't want you nattering in my ear."

"They do know you're a wizard though, don't they? You reek of magic."

"Yes, they know I'm a wizard," said Finn, trying to ignore the way the knocker was sniffing at him again. "They're just… well… it's complicated. *Please*, stay here."

Norm sniffed the air mournfully, but he sat down again, next to the sleeping Tomkin. He patted his round little belly and sighed sadly.

"I'll bring you something back," promised Finn, running a hand through his hair resignedly.

"Hooray!" cried Norm, so enthusiastically Finn suspected the previous sadness had been an act. "I like pasties."

"We don't eat pasties for breakfast," said Finn. "Count yourself lucky if I manage a piece of toast."

Without waiting for a response, Finn strode out, closing his bedroom door firmly behind him.

Five

The Riddle

Thankfully, Finn's parents were happy to chat to each other whilst he stuffed his face with toast. For some reason, he found it very hard to focus on anything other than the fact a talking cat, living garden gnome and letter from a sea princess all waited for him in his bedroom! As food filled his stomach, however, the idea of their presence bothered him less and less. He wasn't sure if it was the effect of the sugary jam or his own madness, but with each mouthful he began to think that a bit of adventure might be just what this holiday needed. Maybe it was *his* turn to arrive back at school with a tale to share instead of being teased for his 'human' holiday. Finn's mind showed him a memory of the laughing faces of his schoolmates as they jeered at him before turning their attention away. They'd then swap their own stories of visits to magical sites and, in the case of Gabe, wild explorations. His father was an explorer, and he was always in far-flung countries investigating mythical stuff. Exactly the sort of things Finn now faced, yet had believed was impossible unless you found yourself up a mountain in Tibet. Yet here he was, with the chance to have his own adventure. One he could talk about. He imagined the eyes of the other boys, all listening to him with surprised interest. The thought was not an unpleasant one.

Once he'd eaten, taking far longer than usual as his imagination conjured scenarios where he became the class hero, Finn returned to his room. When he stepped through the doorway to find his bed empty of mythical creatures, both hope and disappointment flared in his chest. Had it all been a dream after all?

Then, Norm's bearded face popped up from under the little desk in the corner.

"What on earth are you doing under there?" Finn cried after making sure the door was properly shut behind him.

"Exploring," replied Norm, acting as if wriggling

around on the floor was entirely normal. "Food?" he added hopefully.

"Where's the cat?" asked Finn as he pulled out a piece of toast that was rapidly becoming little more than crumbs.

"Under the bed," replied Norm, greedily grabbing Finn's offering. "I don't think he liked it when I bounced." He then proceeded to stuff all the toast into his mouth at once.

Finn had to look away; knockers were evidently *not* neat eaters. His eyes fell on the little bottle again. Taking a determined breath, he picked it up.

"So, can you explain this to me then?" he asked Norm, pulling out the roll of paper and offering it out to Norm.

Swallowing his last morsel with an unreasonably loud slurp, Norm accepted the note with buttery fingers. Clearing his throat, he read. The words sounded even stranger to Finn when spoken in Norm's Cornish accent.

I call for the help of a magical child,
One with the strength to take on the wild.
For centuries now, I've been trapped with no power,
An innocent victim, locked in a tower.

The keys to my chains, so tightly bound,
Will not be simply or easily found.
Two shells are required, but not any will do,
These ones are special, for only a few.
Magical blood is needed to see,
To find them and take them and bring them to me.

One forms a lock in the bonds of a creature,
Whose wonderful voice was her very best feature.
With a scaly long tail and luscious blonde mane,
All that have met her remember her name.
In the village of Zennor, she is waiting and plotting,
Whilst all those that wronged her are endlessly rotting.
She hides in plain sight, with my shell as her cage,
A beauty he might be, but beware of her rage.

The second was claimed as a monster's dear prize.
Tread slowly and carefully, for he's a great size.
His temper's quite awful, don't go in for a fight
Defeat him with logic and cunning, not might
Try not to fear, for he's stupid and vain.
Words and quick thinking will scramble his brain.

When both are collected, bring them to me,
Where I shall be waiting, imprisoned at sea.
My Sea Princess power was taken away,
So with no aid from you, I'll be destined to stay.
Take on this challenge, rescue me do.
I'll forever be thankful, indebted to you.

When he'd finished, Norm looked expectantly up at Finn. "See?" he said.

"I told you, it's not that I can't read it," said Finn in frustration. "It's that it doesn't make sense."

"Well, it's a bit of a riddle in places," admitted Norm, "but the gist is fairly clear."

"And what's that?"

"That this so-called sea princess has been imprisoned and requires two magic shells to set her free."

"Ok…," mused Finn. "And does it say where they might be?"

"Roughly speaking."

"So, all I have to do is find some shells, and I can free her?"

"Yes, but…"

"That doesn't sound so hard," said Finn to himself.

"I don't know, it all sounds terribly tricky to me," said

Norm, his blue eyes wide with fear. "When are you going to throw it back in the sea?"

"Actually," said Finn, making up his mind as he turned the bottle over in his hands. "I think I'm going to help."

"What!" cried Norm, so dramatically you'd have thought Finn had just pronounced he was going to turn into a chicken. "No, no, no. It's far too dangerous."

"But earlier you said I couldn't possibly ignore it!"

"Ah, yes. You'll find I'm very fickle. And I love playing devil's advocate. Trust me, you'll find it unbelievably charming eventually."

"I doubt it," muttered Finn, wondering why, if he had to be tied to a magical creature, it wasn't one who agreed with him and told him how wonderful he was.

"Anyway," Finn declared, more confident than he felt, "I've decided, and that's that."

"But... you're a... *child*." Norm whispered the last word, as if breaking the news to Finn, like Finn had been living under the illusion he was something else.

"I'm sure I can help," Finn pushed on.

"Why don't you give the note to someone more... able? Like a grown-up?"

"No," frowned Finn. "I can do it. Gabe is always doing stuff like this; how hard can it be?"

"Who's Gabe?" quizzed Norm.

"A boy at school. He's the son of a famous wizard explorer, and he's forever solving mysteries and saving people."

"Wow," said Norm, his expression dreamy. "Maybe you should pass this onto him? He sounds a lot more qualified?"

"No!" cried Finn. "I'm the best at magic in my year. I'll be fine. It'll be an adventure," he added, putting as much certainty into his voice as he could muster.

"Uh huh, if you say so," said Norm, raising a single eyebrow.

"You don't have to stick around," snapped Finn. "I can take you back to Men an Tol anytime you want."

"No, no. It'll be… great!" Norm flashed him a less than convincing grin. "We'll help, won't we Tomkin?"

At the mention of his name, Tomkin poked his head out from under Finn's bed, yawning.

"I'm sorry, what were you saying?" he said, stretching his long limbs and giving himself a good scratch before regarding them with a bemused expression.

"I said, we'll help solve the riddle," announced Norm. As he spoke, he clambered onto Finn's chest of drawers. He drew his pickaxe and waved it in the air. "We will embark on this quest and rescue the fair maiden," he continued passionately. "We'll fight off dangerous foes and win untold glory," he cried, clearly so in the swing of things he didn't notice the look of scorn forming on Tomkin's face. "A wizard, a knocker and a cat, all heroes at last!"

"No, I don't think so," said Tomkin when Norm, at last, paused long enough to allow anyone else to speak. "It all sounds a bit too much like hard work. I'm old. I think I'll just lie in the sun. Feel free to let me know how it all goes, though. If you don't die, that is."

"I thought you said you wanted to stay?" said Finn, feeling disappointed he'd lost an ally already.

"Oh, I do, but I'll just watch all the strenuous stuff from a nice, comfy distance, if it's all the same with you."

"Coward," muttered Norm under his breath.

Tomkin ignored him, choosing to return to cleaning his fur.

"Well, anyway," said Finn, trying not to let his enthusiasm lose its momentum. "I'm going to try."

He picked up the letter again and read through it. The words still made little sense, but he could see now that it was a riddle. Grabbing a notebook and pen, he spread them all out on the bed.

"Come on, Norm," he said. "Let's figure this out properly."

"Ok," said Norm, beaming. "Which bit do you want to

look at first? The part about the mermaid or the giant?"

Finn squeaked in alarm.

Tomkin chuckled.

All Finn's hope turned instantly to doubt. He took a steadying breath, but before he'd even finished squashing down his alarm at the mention of yet *more* magical creatures, Mum's voice trilled up the stairs.

"Finn, it's time to go."

"Actually," he said with a sigh, "the first problem I've got to face is the beach."

Six

The Trouble With Sandcastles

Finn had been more than a little nervous allowing Norm into the same room as his parents, despite the knocker's assurances. It only took a second, however, for Finn to realise Norm was right. A dancing, filthy, bearded man spinning around the room shouting, "See, I told you so," was definitely something his parents would have noticed. In fact, the biggest issue for Finn turned out to be controlling his response. It was *very* hard not to laugh as Norm somersaulted across the rug, climbed up the curtains and blew a loud raspberry in Dad's ear.

"What's so funny?" Mum quizzed him as Finn

attempted to straighten his face.

"Nothing, nothing. Just excited about the beach."

"Oh, great," said Mum. "Hurry and get your stuff then."

"I wouldn't go in the water if I were you," called Norm from where he was swinging, "not with that morgawr about."

It took everything Finn had not to answer. Instead, he simply nodded to Mum and ran back upstairs to retrieve a towel from the airing cupboard. In the entrance to his room, he spotted Tomkin.

"Aren't you coming?" Finn whispered.

"I won't be invisible to them," he explained. "There's too much 'normal' cat in me. They won't be able to hear me speak, but I've learned over the years that humans are not overly tolerant of unexpected animals in their homes."

"No, they wouldn't," said Finn, relieved Tomkin had stayed hidden.

"I'll make my own way, if I must." He narrowed his eyes at Finn. "I really don't like sand, you know."

"You don't have to come," said Finn. "It probably won't be very interesting."

"No," sighed Tomkin. "If you're going to be planning this ridiculous quest, then you'll need *someone* with brains. Also, if you got eaten by a morgawr whilst I was happily sleeping on your bed, I'd never forgive myself. Well," he considered, tilting his head, "not for a week or two, anyway."

The beach, when they got there, was as horrendous as always, with hundreds of families spread out across the sand. At least this time Finn had someone to talk to, although he had to make sure he kept his voice down. Unable to see Norm, they'd assume he was talking to himself, which wasn't a good look in the human world. Thankfully, no one appeared interested in him as he lay out his towel on a spot as far from any listening ears as possible.

Pulling the riddle from his pocket, he sat down to study it again, crossing his bare legs and resting the paper in his lap. A notch formed on his brow as he read, his light brown hair flopping forward as he bent closer and closer to the page. He muttered the words under his breath, hearing them in Norm's voice. The Cornish accent somehow helped with the understanding of the puzzle. Now Norm had said the word 'mermaid', the description of the creature with a scaly tail and mane of blonde hair made far more sense. Which part referred to a giant, however, remained a mystery.

Doubt clawed at him as he wondered if he truly wanted to embark on this particular adventure after all. He couldn't go back on his declaration, though, not without looking like a cowardly idiot. He squared his shoulders and took a deep breath.

"So," he said to Norm, "you mentioned something about mermaids and giants before? You mean a real mermaid and giant, don't you? It's not code for something?"

"Code? No," laughed Norm with a shake of the head. "It says that they each have one of these shells. That's who we need to take them from."

"Take?" said Finn in alarm. "I'm not sure that's the right attitude. I really don't want to steal from a giant."

"What, you think you can just ask nicely and he'll give it to you?" asked Tomkin with a smirk. He'd slunk onto the beach only moments after they'd arrived and was now taking up way more than his fair share of the towel.

Finn huffed in response, guessing the cat was correct in his scepticism.

"I wouldn't get het up about the giant for now," said Norm. "Technically, that's the second shell. Why don't we ignore it for now? The worry might go away if we don't think about it."

"I'm not convinced that's true," said Finn.

"Works for me!" insisted Norm jovially.

Finn rolled his eyes.

"Fine," he agreed, running a hand through his hair.

He'd forgotten his hat, and his scalp was already tingling in the heat. "Is a mermaid less dangerous then?"

"Oh no," chuckled Norm. He'd taken his boots and socks off, and was experimentally wiggling his toes in the sand. His very hairy toes, Finn noted. "They can be ferocious," Norm continued. "And Morveren is known for being quite lethal."

"Who's Morveren?"

"The mermaid of Zennor. The one who's got the first shell."

"Great." Finn crossed his arms grumpily.

"No one's heard of her for years, though. Rumour has it she was killed, probably by those humans she used to torment."

"Then how can we get the shell off her?" Finn was feeling more hopeless by the second.

"Oh, I'm sure she just hid it somewhere." He took his hat off now, propping it under his head and lying back in imitation of the hundreds of other sunbathers. Only the coal dust smattered over him ruined the illusion. Finn mentally reminded himself to offer the knocker a bath later.

"Fine, let's definitely go with the mermaid first then," resolved Finn. "Tell me everything you know about her."

Before Norm could reply, a shadow fell over them.

Squinting up into the sun, he saw the figure of a girl standing before him.

"You brought your cat to the beach."

It wasn't a question. Finn didn't know how to respond, so he remained silent.

"Doesn't it hate water? I thought all cats hated water?"

"He's a little… unusual," said Finn, forcing himself to ignore Norm's fit of giggles. Instead, he kept his focus on the girl, who was wrinkling her freckled nose as if trying to solve some complex puzzle. Then, in a flash, her concern evaporated and she shrugged.

"Cool," she said, smiling so widely Finn could see she was missing her two top teeth.

She looked about the same age as him, but probably a good head taller. Finn knew he was short and was always envious of those that towered over him. She wore a swimming costume, like almost everyone else around them, and it was wet. Salt had dried on her skin, and water dripped from the end of two reddish brown plaits, messily braided, which framed her tanned face. Blue eyes smiled down at him, dimples forming on her cheeks as she waited patiently for a response.

Normally, Finn would have jumped at the chance to talk to someone who didn't want to ridicule him, but he had more important things to do.

"Can I help you with something?" he said coldly. It pained him to be so rude, to keep his face stony as he watched the smile slip from hers.

"Oh… no," she mumbled, turning to leave. "Sorry."

"She seemed nice," said Norm, once the girl had left. "You were a bit mean though."

"We've got a rescue mission to plan," said Finn, pushing down his feelings of guilt. "Now, tell me what you know about this mermaid."

"She's very famous. *Everyone's* heard of her, even the humans. She stole the heart of a man and dragged him away from his bride and into the sea."

"She sounds lovely," said Finn.

"No, she was quite awful," corrected Norm, obviously not understanding Finn's sarcasm.

"But she lived in Zennor?" asked Finn.

"Probably," said Norm. He was sitting up again now, studying Finn's bucket with interest. "How do you make a sandcastle?" he added.

Finn frowned. "You just fill up the bucket with sand and then tip it over," he said. "But the mermaid, what happened to her?"

"No idea," replied Norm, although Finn had the

suspicion he wasn't really focusing anymore. He'd found the spade and was scooping up sand with it, examining it closely as he poured it into the bucket.

"Do mermaids have particularly long lives?" he pushed.

"No, not particularly. No longer than a hundred years or so, anyway."

"So, she'll definitely be long dead by now?" asked Finn, feeling the need to confirm this again.

Norm shrugged as he continued to dig. Once the bucket was full, he turned it over with a flourish. He held his breath as he lifted it up expectantly. All the sand tumbled out in an untidy pile.

"Hmm, tricky," he muttered to himself before grabbing the spade and starting all over again.

Finn watched, but his mind was on the mermaid. If she was dead, like he hoped, then his task was to find where she'd hidden the shell. This wasn't without its problems, though. Firstly, being a mermaid, she could well have left it in the sea. There was no way he could search there. He could barely swim in a swimming pool.

But, he reasoned with himself, if it was in the sea, surely the sea princess would have been able to get it herself, or at least find some other water creature to do it for her? If she needed Finn, then logic told him the shell *must* be hidden on the land somewhere. That meant only one thing.

"Norm?" he said. "Where exactly is Zennor?"

Finn braced himself for the reply, fearing it would be at the other end of the country.

"Oh, about an hour away in one of your vehicle things you travel about in," he said, not bothering to look up from his sandy work.

"What? Seriously? That close?"

"Why?" asked Tomkin. "Are you thinking of going there and just, what? Looking around in the hope you'll find this shell?" His disdain was obvious.

"Well, yes," admitted Finn. "Do you have a better idea?"

"Not one that doesn't involve hours of research and effort, so, no, your plan is as good as any."

"Right, ok then," said Finn, unnerved by Tomkin's approval. "I'll go and see if my mum and dad will take me there."

Without waiting to hear any more words of questionable encouragement, Finn ran up the beach to where his parents sat.

"Mum? Dad?" he called. "Could we have another day out tomorrow?"

"Finn?" asked Mum, not listening to him but peering

past him over her sunglasses. "Why is there a cat on your beach towel?"

Finn glanced over his shoulder and saw Tomkin stretching out to his full length.

"Um… he… er… he… belongs to one of the neighbours," Finn lied clumsily. "He's rather befriended me."

"Hmm, well, don't let him in the house," she ordered. "Now, what did you want?"

"I was just reading about Zennor and wondered if we could go there?"

"Zennor? The place with the mermaid legend?"

He paused, uneasy at the mention of something magical. He knew he'd have to proceed carefully.

"Yes," he said slowly.

"They're not real, are they?" she asked in a horrified whisper, but only after glancing around to make sure no one could overhear her.

Beside her, Dad dropped his book and waited for Finn's response.

"No," he lied again, forcing out a little fake laugh. "No. I just heard it was a… a really beautiful village."

He smiled serenely, making himself look as innocent as possible under their suspicious gazes. He couldn't blame them; he wouldn't have believed him either.

"Ok. Yes," Mum agreed after an awkward moment. "I had noticed it mentioned in a few guidebooks. It's got a rather lovely church, by all accounts. We could go tomorrow?"

She turned to Dad, who nodded, but without taking his eyes off Finn.

"I think that should be possible," he said.

"Great," said Finn.

They all fell silent again, before Finn backed away.

"I think I'll get back to my sandcastles," he said, trying to sound casual.

"I can take you for a swim in a minute?" offered Dad.

"NO!" His cry was so loud and dramatic that Dad jumped about a foot in the air. "I mean, no thank you. I just… I'm really into my sandcastles at the moment."

"That's great," beamed Dad, seemingly delighted Finn was enjoying something normal for once. "I'll come and see what you've made after I've finished my chapter."

"Can't wait," said Finn, his fake smile stretching so tight now his face was beginning to ache. As he turned, he scowled, kicking the sand. Now he'd actually have to make a stupid sandcastle.

"You're a terrible liar, you know that right?" commented Tomkin when Finn got back, his large ears evidently having heard the whole conversation.

"Thanks," muttered Finn. His mood didn't improve when he saw what Norm had created in his absence.

"These sandcastles aren't as easy as they look," he said from where he stood, at the bottom of a hole that looked like it was trying to swallow him up. All around lay pathetically small piles of sand that resembled anything but castles.

Sighing, Finn picked up a spade and got to work.

Seven

Zennor

The drive to Zennor took slightly longer than Norm had predicted. Partly because they got stuck behind a tractor, and partly because Dad couldn't drive faster than a snail down the narrow Cornish roads.

"Are we almost there yet?" Finn asked for the hundredth time.

Normally, long journeys didn't bother him, but then normally he didn't have a talking cat hiding in his backpack, getting crosser and crosser with every second that passed. When they finally pulled into a very bumpy car park, Tomkin let out a small *miaow* of frustration.

"What was that Finn?" asked Mum, turning slightly in her seat.

"Oh, nothing, just yawning," he said, stretching his face into a fake yawn as he gave his bag a warning poke. She frowned at him, yet didn't push the point, which Finn took as a win.

"Poke me again and I'll eat your fingers," growled Tomkin.

Getting out of the car, the first thing Finn noticed was the wind. It whipped at him, blowing his t-shirt up and his mousy hair in every direction.

"It's quite exposed," commented Dad, pointing out the wildly obvious.

"Oo, look, that cafe does cream teas," said Mum, gesturing to a sign attached to the side of an old, stone barn.

That was the good thing about Cornwall, you could always be guaranteed a cream tea, even in the most remote of places. Finn didn't care if it was jam or cream that got splodged on first, it was utterly delicious. His stomach gave a rumble in anticipation, but a hiss from Tomkin and cough from Norm stopped him mindlessly following his parents towards the cafe.

"Can we have a look around first?" he asked. "Maybe see the church?"

Finn had no interest in churches, but from the little he could find out about the mermaid of Zennor, or Morveren as Norm kept referring to her, the church was the centre of the drama. It had been from there the human man had been stolen. It also housed a carving of her, set in an old wooden bench. It seemed the best place to start.

"Then we could have a cream tea afterwards?" Finn added, not willing to deny his stomach, even for the glory of adventure.

"Alright," agreed Mum.

"I need to stretch my legs anyway," said Dad.

The church was only a stone's throw from the carpark. Finn carried his backpack very carefully until he could find somewhere to release Tomkin away from prying eyes. He was all too conscious of the cat's sharp claws that could definitely puncture fabric and scratch him if desired. The sun was bright and hot, despite the wind, and quite a few people were milling about, taking photographs of the church, or themselves.

As they passed the pub, Norm let out a squeal of delight.

"He looks like me," he cried, pointing at the sign swinging in the breeze.

True enough, the miner painted on the board had a

very knocker-ish look about him, with a miner's hat and full beard.

"Stay focused," ordered Finn as Norm tried to copy the man's pose, waving his pickaxe around and almost slicing Finn's kneecaps open.

With a sigh, Finn decided to ignore him and focus instead on studying everything he passed intently, searching for anything that might be a clue. The scene, however, offered nothing. Not that Finn knew what he was looking for. The shell was hardly going to be waiting for him under a neon sign.

The village itself was so small, Finn was expecting the church to be magnificent to warrant the number of visitors there. Yet, it appeared to be no different from any other his parents had forced him to over the years. It was pretty enough, he supposed as they climbed up the steep steps that led to the entrance, if you liked that sort of thing. Evidently Mum and Dad did, as they started to "oo" and "ah" at each other, reading aloud from their guidebook and generally acting like they were visiting the eighth wonder of the world.

Approaching the front door, Finn noticed that most of the people he could see were now heading towards the cafe or the pub, the hour of the day calling them to get food. Ignoring his own pang of hunger, he wandered inside.

He felt the drop in temperature immediately. A shiver ran through him, and Norm moved closer to his side.

"I think we're in the right place," Norm muttered. Finn didn't question what he meant, he had the same feeling. He couldn't put his finger on how he knew, but something in the air felt magical. In the same way as you can tell when a thunderstorm is coming.

Making the most of the dull light, and the fact his parents were still outside examining the stonework, Finn bent down and quickly released Tomkin.

"Stay out of sight," he whispered, but his warning was unnecessary. The cat immediately slunk into the shadows, his brown markings camouflaging perfectly. The church was mainly empty. The few people there were all gathered around a wooden bench off to his right.

"I'm guessing that's the carving," he said.

Norm nodded, and they made their way forwards, waiting for their 'turn'. It was quite a tiny church, and his parents appeared beside him a second later.

"This was a great call Finn," said Dad. "Did you know the church was probably built on top of a Celtic site from the Stone Age?"

"Hmm," responded Finn, not really listening. He'd reached the bench, the group in front having moved on, and was frozen to the spot. He stared, not believing what his eyes were showing him. The photograph he'd studied in the guidebook had shown a fairly plain and rustic wooden carving. Nice enough, but certainly *not* what he was currently looking at.

What he saw was a smooth slab of wood, meticulously inlaid with hundreds of pieces of shell and sea glass. The mermaid they formed shimmered, despite the lack of light inside the church. Her black, glass eyes shone and danced with life. As Finn gawped, he thought he could hear the sound of the waves crashing and a lilting voice singing sweetly. He shook his head to clear it and glanced at Norm. To his relief, the knocker looked just as mesmerised as he felt.

"She looks so real," Norm whispered.

As Finn turned his gaze back, this time studying further than the mermaid's bewitching eyes, he noticed what she held in her hand. Bigger than any of the others, this shell also shone more brightly. Iridescent colours danced over its ridged, white surface, calling to be touched.

"I think we've found what we came for," he whispered.

The mermaid seemed to smile in response, and Finn straightened quickly.

"How quaint," said Mum from behind him. The

mythical story of Morveren was the least interesting thing about this place to his parents, despite Finn's assurances mermaids weren't real. Even as a story, it was too close to magic for their liking. Historical facts were far more comfortable.

As Finn stood and continued to stare, his parents moved off to inspect the altar, far more suited to their tastes.

"What do we do now?" Finn asked Norm.

Norm glanced around.

"Wait till it's empty and try to take it, I guess," he suggested. His tone, however, was far from confident, and Finn didn't feel great about the idea either. As ludicrous as it sounded, the mermaid was far too alive for his liking. She seemed to watch him, and laughter echoed in his ears. If she was as evil as the stories suggested, and she wanted him to take the shell, then was it really sensible?

"We're going to have a look at the graveyard," he heard Dad say. "Coming Finn?"

"I'll be out in a second," he replied, not daring to take his eyes from the shell. He heard them walk away.

"We're alone," whispered Tomkin, slinking around the side of the bench.

"Do it quickly," ordered Norm.

Before his nerves could get the better of him, Finn

stretched out, grasping the shell with his fingertips. He'd expected it to be stuck solid, for his fingers to slip off with nothing in them. When the shell practically fell into his palm, he almost laughed with shock and delight. That was until the church door thudded shut and a crazed cackle boomed around the space. Any light that had been coming in the windows was suddenly blotted out, as if dark clouds had been summoned.

"Uh oh! Maybe that wasn't such a good idea," said Norm.

"So adept at pointing out the obvious, as usual," snapped Tomkin.

Finn didn't say a word. He couldn't do anything but hold his breath as the sound of splintering wood chilled him to the bone. To his horror, the bejewelled torso of the mermaid was moving, shells and glass flaking away to reveal mottled green skin. Norm gave a shrill scream as a face jutted forward, breaking free to take a dry gasp of air.

"Freedom," croaked a voice that resembled the sucking of waves over pebbles. Morveren's eyes looked without really seeing, jumping from object to object like a buzzing fly. "Free, after centuries. Free, and able to take my revenge."

Finn felt an overwhelming sense that now would be the moment to leave. He took a single step to the side.

Unfortunately, Norm had also chosen that moment to depart. They bumped into each other, not hard, but enough to cause Finn to stumble and topple to the floor. As if suddenly illuminated by a spotlight, Morveren's full attention pivoted to him at once. Mad fury radiated outwards.

"Free," she hissed, "to kill my oppressors and destroy my prison."

Finn opened his mouth to defend himself.

"I didn't… I haven't…" was all he got out before a cold wetness leached into his body. As he glanced downwards, he saw water was trickling from somewhere. It pooled around him, glowing eerily green, as if he needed any evidence it was magical!

Hurriedly, he got to his feet, but the water was rising so quickly it had already passed his knees. Morveren clearly didn't care about his innocence.

"Time to leave?" said Tomkin, appearing through an alcove above the bench. "Cats don't swim you know, even fairy ones."

"Nor do knockers," added Norm, attempting to climb up Finn's leg.

Finn didn't need telling twice. Picking Norm up, with some difficulty as he wasn't exactly light, he waded towards the entrance. Tomkin followed, leaping elegantly from pew to pew. When they reached the solid wooden doors, Finn yanked on the handle.

Nothing.

He pushed and pulled, rattling it with all his might. Norm banged too, and Tomkin shouted less than helpful instructions.

"Pull harder!"

"Hurry up!"

"Lift the latch!"

"It won't budge," cried Finn.

The water was at his chest now, and panic was setting in. Around him, shadows and shapes swam, at which he didn't dare look at too closely. The light was spreading up the walls. As it reached the ceiling, Finn heard Morveren cry with glee. A wave descended, crashing down on their heads with a force that had Finn spinning and somersaulting backwards. For a moment, he didn't know which way was up. Norm was ripped from his arms, and he saw a tangle of fur slide past, which he assumed was Tomkin. Then other sights forced themselves upon him. Shoals of fish. An octopus with tentacles that tangled around his limbs momentarily before moving on. His clothes billowed as he struggled to fight his fear and think.

Still, he heard Morveren's laughter.

Desperately, he swam towards the sound. By the time he reached her, his lungs were burning.

Please, he attempted to mouth. *I'm innocent.*

Finn wasn't sure if she could understand him, but she studied him intently. Then his vision blurred. Strange images flashed before him. Initially, they rattled past so quickly he couldn't make any sense of them, but eventually they slowed.

A man stood in the very church Finn floated in. He was collecting bibles, stacking them neatly, when he paused. A song on the air drifted in, an enchanting melody pulling him out into the crisp night. He didn't stop once, just strode unseeing all the way down to the sea. The tide was high, and a golden head was bobbing amongst the waves, singing sweetly. Without a hesitation, the man waded into the water. He opened his mouth and joined in with the song, his own voice beautiful too. His lips still moved even as the sea engulfed him, filling him up and choking out his life, all as he stared in wonder at the mermaid.

Finn didn't have a chance to cry out in alarm before the scene disappeared, another smoothly taking its place. It still showed the sea, but the mermaid was alone now. All was peaceful until, in a flash, nets descended, surrounding her. She kicked her strong tail, but it was too late. The nets closed in, tangling her in rough knots. Screaming in rage, Morveren struggled helplessly as hands reached down and dragged her into the air.

The image changed again. This time, a group of humans carried Morveren, a gag tied tightly over her mouth, into a dark cave. They all stopped inside the entrance, nervousness dripping from them. One man, holding a basket of fish, stepped forward at last.

"King Carraba," he called out, shaking with fear. "Mighty god of the shoreline, please honour us with an audience."

Finn found himself waiting, as tense as the men. Then, a boom echoed from deep within the darkness.

"Who summons me?"

"Faithful worshippers from the village of Zennor. We beg for your help in dealing with one who has wronged us greatly."

"Do you bring an offering?" the voice asked, getting louder.

"Yes. And we'll bring more. Whatever you wish in return for your help."

A strange scuttling reverberated, echoing off the rocks,

before its source appeared. The creature was so large it towered over the men and scraped along the roof of the cave. A giant crab, its spiked shell curved like a crown, with two protruding eyes on stalks that peered down.

"What help do you require?"

"We want this abomination punished for what she did," answered the man, as another behind him thrust Morveren forwards.

"And what did she do?"

"She stole a man. And killed him."

The crab thing, Carraba, considered them all for a moment.

"Bring me one hundred fish for one hundred nights and I will give you what you need to punish her."

"Agreed," said the man holding the basket. He then put down his basket, slopping with its offering, and pulled out a blade. Pricking his finger, he allowed a drop of blood to fall to the ground where it soaked into the sand. "I swear it," he declared.

Behind him, all the other humans took out their blades and mirrored his actions and words.

"Good," announced Carraba, satisfied. "Now, do as I say."

A nervous anticipation hung in the air as the humans

leaned in to listen.

"Entomb her in wood," continued Carraba. "Be sure to keep her alive. Once sealed, secure this shell in the surface."

A pincer came forward, the clam shell it clutched tiny in comparison.

"It will lock her in. She'll be forever doomed to see but not move, witness life but not live it. Does that sound like punishment enough?"

"It does," gasped the man, awestruck as he leaned forward and took the shell. The very same one Finn now clutched in his hand.

Then next set of images were so traumatic Finn could hardly bear to watch. Morveren, screaming and writhing, was trapped in the bench. A circle, mocking carving was placed on top of her, muffling her fury, before the shell was rested against the wood. It shone brightly for a second, then went dull, fused in position. All went silent.

Once the scenes had finished, Finn was left staring at Morveren, feeling slightly sick. Her eyes, dark coals in her head, burned with vengeance.

It wasn't me, he mouthed.

"I don't care," she hissed back.

He felt the last of his oxygen dwindle, and lights popped in his vision. He tried to turn, to find Norm and Tomkin, to be with them in his final moments, but his body wouldn't obey his commands. A pounding had started in his head, painfully loud. To begin with, he thought it was the sound of his heart, struggling to beat with no air to feed it. Then, he realised it was coming from outside his body. With a monumental effort, he pivoted, his eyes widening when he located the source of the noise. Norm, suspended in the flood, was attacking the closed doors with his pickaxe. Each swing landed with less force than the last, yet he grimaced with steely determination. As Finn gaped, a small crack developed. Then a chunk of wood splintered away. Liquid leaked out of the gap, and a gentle current built around Finn, pulling his body forward.

But it wasn't enough. Unconsciousness took hold of him. Strange sounds resounded in his head; laughter, a sweet song and a tearing of something very, very far away. He let himself get carried on a stream of movement, lulling him to sleep.

The darkness was about to win when a jerk threw him violently forwards, his limbs flailing uncontrollably. Then he crashed down, hard stone slamming against his skin and warm air flooding his lungs. He shuddered with pain and relief, unwilling to open his eyes and find out if he was dead or alive. When he finally summoned the courage, the sight that met him left him dizzy with shock. He lay on the ground outside the church, the wooden doors hanging loosely on their hinges, and through them poured a green light. It washed over him, cold and wet but more mist than water now. Flowing down the steps, it journeyed over the roof of the pub and across the fields, disappearing in the direction of the sea. Shimmering images of fish and other creatures swam amongst it, iridescent in the sunshine. When the last of it faded into the horizon, Finn heard a distant sigh travel back to him on the breeze.

The sea. I'm home.

Finn couldn't help but feel glad.

"Well, that was all rather dramatic," declared Norm, popping up from inside a bush and shaking droplets from his beard like a dog.

"Next time I say I'm not coming, I mean it," said Tomkin, stalking out of another patch of foliage.

"You're both ok!" cried Finn in happiness, his relief drawing him out of his trance.

"No thanks to you," grumbled Tomkin. "I can't believe I'm now indebted to a knocker. How embarrassing!"

"You were amazing, Norm," agreed Finn.

Norm blushed brightly and gave a little bow, flourishing his hat.

"It's an honour to serve," he said, a delighted smile stretching over his face.

"Do you at least have the damn shell?" asked Tomkin, putting an end to the emotional scene.

Finn opened his clasped hand and stretched it out to show them. The shell was about the size of his palm, dull in the daylight. Whatever gleam it had possessed whilst in the bench had gone, and it looked totally ordinary. The rough grooves that ran over it had the faintest tinge of pink. Inside, it was as smooth as glass, pleasant to the touch. Finn could only assume the second shell would be its pair.

"It's not very impressive for a powerful magical object, is it?" scorned Tomkin.

Finn couldn't argue, but he felt no doubt it was the right shell. Not after witnessing Morveren's memories. His fingers tingled.

"Put it somewhere safe," ordered Norm, glancing around. "You never know who might be watching."

Finn had just tucked the shell into the pocket of his shorts when his parents wandered around the side of the church, having finished their inspection of the graveyard. It was only then, when he saw their mouths open in shock, that Finn realised he was dripping wet.

They stood motionless in disbelief, staring at him.

Mum closed her eyes momentarily, muttering something to herself under her breath. Dad pinched the bridge of his nose.

Finn waited.

"We don't want to know, do we?" Mum asked, her expression pained.

"Probably not," admitted Finn, a single drip running down his forehead, all the way to his chin.

"Let's go and get something to eat," sighed Dad.

Eight

The Girl

Mum and Dad led the way, Finn padding behind them, his sandals leaving a trail of wet footprints. Before entering the cafe, Dad grabbed a towel from the car and made Finn sit on it, like some mud-covered dog. The cafe owners laughed at him, and made jokes about investing in some swimming trunks before his next visit to the beach. Finn tried to grin sheepishly, but the tension rolling off his parents was enough to make his scone and cream taste sour.

The silence on the journey home was even worse.

"You should ask them if we can go to St. Agnes tomorrow," suggested Norm. "If I remember correctly, that's where the giant lives."

"Are you joking?" whispered Finn, bending his head low so Mum and Dad couldn't see his lips move. "After today, I'm seriously re-thinking everything."

"Wisest thing you've said since we met," muttered Tomkin from Finn's bag, where he'd reluctantly returned after Finn had emerged from the cafe.

"But today was a victory," argued Norm.

"We almost died!" hissed Finn.

"Not really," shrugged Norm. "Well, ok, yes, you're right. We almost died, true, but… we didn't, did we? And we got the shell. So… an overall win I'd say."

Finn shook his head.

"I think he might have inhaled too much water and it's affected his already questionable brain," said Tomkin. "I say we chuck the first bit of shell into the sea, the note with it, and pretend the whole thing never happened."

Norm looked horrified at the very suggestion.

"Finn would never do that, would you Finn?"

"I don't know," whispered Finn, "but whatever I do, it won't be tomorrow. I need to at least *try* and act normal for one day, otherwise my parents might actually lose the plot."

Norm glanced up at them then, the stiffness of their spins a clear indication of their continued stress.

"Maybe a day of sandcastles wouldn't be a bad idea," he agreed.

The next day, that's exactly what they did.

Finn had tried to act as if nothing odd had happened all evening, but every time his parents looked at him, questions they didn't dare ask formed behind their eyes. In the end, Finn had gone to bed early, tucking the shell under his pillow for safe keeping. When he'd gone down to breakfast to find the guidebooks firmly closed on the side, he'd known all was not forgotten. When Dad suggested the local beach, Finn had nodded enthusiastically.

So, he'd spent the morning watching as Norm delighted in making more and more sandcastles. He'd got the hang of them now, selecting the perfect sand and packing it firmly into the bucket before tipping it over with a dramatic flourish. After a few taps with the spade, he shimmied the bucket up and away to reveal the results. His success rate was pretty good, and he'd started to create rings of them, all joining together to create a super castle.

"You could live it in," joked Finn.

Initially, he'd been worried that the other beach goers,

unable to see Norm, would see the bucket moving on its own. Norm, however, had reassured him the magic that made him invisible extended to the objects he held too. It also caused people to look away, and for their brains to fill in the blanks.

"So," he told Finn, "as long as you're here making them too, everyone will assume this is your wonderful creation."

This didn't exactly fill Finn with joy. Having to spend a day on his hands and knees getting covered in sand was something he'd tried to avoid at all costs.

"Rather you than me," yawned Tomkin, who'd stretched out in the very centre of the towel, as far from Norm and his slightly haphazard method of digging as possible.

"That's really cool," said a voice after Finn and Norm had been building for some time.

Squinting up, Finn saw a girl. It was the one from before. The one who seemed all too keen to be friendly.

"Thanks," he said, looking away again at once, not wanting to offer any sign of invitation.

"It would look even better with some shells to decorate it," she went on, either ignoring his rudeness or not noticing it. "I can collect some if you like?"

"No thanks," answered Finn. "I like working alone."

"Oh." She sounded disappointed, but still didn't leave.

Norm looked from Finn to the girl.

"She could help," he said. "It *would* look good with shells."

"No," muttered Finn, as quietly as he could. Not quietly enough, apparently.

"Did you say something?" the girl asked.

"No," Finn frowned at her.

"You don't have any brothers or sisters either, do you?" she went on. "It can get lonely, can't it?"

"No," said Finn again.

"This is really rather awkward," grimaced Norm. "I think she wants to be your friend."

Finn scowled at him, and wished he could tell him to shut up.

"Finn!"

Mum's shout caused Finn to look up. She was waving a sandwich in the air, a sign that it was lunchtime.

"I've got to go," he said to the girl, relieved to have an excuse to leave, as she showed no sign of going herself.

To his surprise, however, she followed him.

"What are you doing?" he asked.

She wasn't looking at him, however. She was smiling at a man and a woman who were sitting suspiciously close to his own parents.

"I'm hungry," the girl said to them. "Is it time for our lunch too?"

"Oh, you two have met, how lovely," said the woman.

Mum and Dad were beaming at him. Finn got a sinking feeling in his stomach as he took his sandwich.

"Finn, this is Mr and Mrs Burnett," said Dad. "They're staying in a house up the road from us."

Finn forced himself to smile politely, but sat down without a word, as far from the girl as he could.

"Beth has been so lonely this week," said Mrs Burnett, supplying the girl with a name. "I'm so glad she's found a friend."

Finn opened his mouth to argue, but when he realised his response would only sound horrible, he simply bit into his sandwich instead.

"We were just arranging a day out together tomorrow," said Mum. "Won't that be fun?"

Finn almost choked on his sandwich.

"But… but…" he spluttered.

Mum glared at him. He swallowed hard and averted his eyes.

"We thought you kids might like to choose where," piped up Mr Burnett, missing the silent exchange between Finn and his mum. "There are lots of beautiful places to see, but we could be convinced to go to an amusement park, I'm sure."

Finn shuddered at the thought, although Beth laughed in delight.

"Suggest St. Agnes," said Norm, nudging Finn in the ribs. He'd followed Finn up the beach and was now attempting to steal a bite of his sandwich. Finn held it higher as he gulped, but compelled himself to speak up.

"I've read St. Agnes is nice," he said, trying to sound innocent. "Lots of mining history."

Mr and Mrs Burnett looked slightly taken aback by his suggestion, and his parents eyed him suspiciously. In front of others, however, they couldn't openly question his motives. Dad gave a fake little laugh.

"Our Finn is very into his books," he explained. "Always reading, this one."

His tone was light, but Finn couldn't help but hear the criticism that laced the words.

"Well, nothing wrong with that," said Mr Burnett. "Makes a nice change from meeting kids obsessed with video games. And St. Agnes sounds like a grand idea."

Mrs Burnett added her approval, Beth nodding along merrily too. Finn beamed, Norm doing a little unseen jig beside him. Only his parents appeared unconvinced, but they shoved down their unease and grinned along with everyone else.

"Hooray for Finn," cried Norm.

Distracted by his achievement, Finn realised too late that he'd let his arm drop. Norm launched, mouth open wide, biting down.

Finn barely let go before he lost his fingers.

"I'm not coming," called Tomkin, ignoring Finn's stifled cry of alarm and stalking past them all, heading back towards the holiday cottage.

"We'll see," retorted Norm, gulping down Finn's sandwich in a single swallow.

That evening, Finn went to his room early again, but this time it was to plan. He poured over the riddle, going through every word with Norm. And Tomkin when he deigned to wake for long enough to help.

"So, you're sure Bolster is a giant?" he asked.

Unfortunately, Norm was in one of his distracted moods. Rather than give Finn his full attention, he was trying to balance on one leg, on top of his hat, which he'd placed in the middle of the room.

"He's not, say, a loveable puppy?" Finn pushed on.

Norm laughed, wobbling. "No, he's a ferocious giant that likes to feast on young girls. Or marry them. I get muddled."

"What!" cried Finn. "You never mentioned that before."

"Didn't I?" mused Norm. "Are you sure?"

"Yes. I would definitely have remembered that!"

"Oh, well, I wouldn't worry. None of us are girls."

"That's hardly the point."

"When you die, do you think your parents will adopt me?" asked Tomkin, from where he lounged on Finn's bed.

"You're coming," said Norm, toppling to the floor. "You owe me, remember. What if we need your help?"

"Yes," added Finn. "What if the way to beat the giant is to insult him? We'd never manage that without you."

"Rude!" growled Tomkin. "Just because you're facing imminent death, there's no need to take it out on me."

"It'll be fine," said Norm, clambering onto his hat once more. "The giants in Cornwall have been asleep for years. Centuries. We just need to find his stash of treasure."

"Well that doesn't sound easy either. How big is St. Agnes?"

"Hmm, you know, village sized," he answered. "It's got a beach too, and cliffs."

"Then how am I *ever* going to find the shell? Zennor was pretty simple. The carved mermaid was a pretty obvious clue, it turned out, but where do we even start looking for a giant's treasure trove?"

"I'm sure we'll figure it out."

Norm sounded very confident, but Finn didn't share the feeling. Especially as, at that moment, the knocker slipped backwards, rolled halfway across the room, banged into the bedside table and caused the lamp to fall on him with a crash.

"Yes, it'll be a roaring success," said Tomkin.

Nine

The Search For Treasure

The journey to St. Agnes the next day was much shorter than the trek down to Zennor had been. Although this was good for Tomkin, zipped up in Finn's bag again, it wasn't so good for Finn's nerves. Despite Norm's assurances, he couldn't help but worry that this Bolster might not be as asleep as he was meant to be. After the unexpected awakening of Morveren, Finn wasn't going to take any chances. He'd already decided that, at the first sign of danger, he was going to abandon the mission entirely.

Pulling into a carpark, it was only when he saw another car, with Beth and her family climbing out of it, that he remembered the other obstacle he'd face that day; getting rid of Beth. She waved far too enthusiastically at him.

"Finn," hissed Mum. "Be polite!"

Dutifully, Finn waved back, but he didn't even try to smile. This girl was just far too annoying.

They all trekked to the beach together, joining droves of other tourists, all searching for the perfect patch of sand to sit on.

"This beach is tiny," commented Finn. He was actually talking to Norm but, of course, Beth wasn't to know that.

"The tide's out though," she replied. "Look, there's another cove around there. We could go and explore?"

"Hmm," murmured Finn. Bitterly, he thought it *did* look like the perfect place to start his search.

"Caves would be a good place to start," said Norm, confirming Finn's hunch.

"Beach shoes on first Finn," called Mum. "I don't want you slipping on the rocks."

Finn rolled his eyes, but did as he was told. There was no point pretending he wouldn't slip, even with the help of rubber shoes. His natural balance was non-existent.

"We should go swimming too," suggested Beth.

"No," replied Finn, far too quickly.

"Finn doesn't seem to like the sea," explained Dad,

noticing the confused look shared by Beth and her parents.

"Oh, that's ok," said Beth with an unconcerned shrug. "We can just explore."

"You can swim instead if you'd prefer?" suggested Finn hopefully.

"No, it's ok," she replied.

Finn tried not to sigh too loudly in disappointment.

"Come on then," he grumbled.

The rocks were slippery, and their progress was slow. Finn attempted to study the cliffs, looking out for any crevices, but the reality was he had to exert such an effort not to fall that he could barely see anything other than his own feet.

"Do you see any caves?" he whispered to Norm.

"I don't think so."

Tomkin had appeared, having kept his distance since being released in the carpark. He pranced easily from rock to rock.

"Is that the same cat you had with you in Falmouth?" asked Beth, having noticed him.

"Er, no," lied Finn, unconvincingly.

Thankfully, Beth didn't question him further, although she raised an eyebrow, a half-smile forming a dimple on one cheek. Finn didn't notice, however, as he slid onto his bottom at that moment and was rather distracted by Norm's cackles of laughter.

The cove, when they reached it, offered more possibilities, but the small caves were soon explored and shown to offer nothing.

"What if I'm missing something?" he asked Norm when Beth had moved out of earshot.

"I reckon your magical blood would help you see anything relevant," he said.

"Unless it's something really meant to be hidden," added Tomkin unhelpfully.

"Well, what do you suggest I do then?" Finn snapped in irritation.

Tomkin thought for a moment.

"The cliffs," he said at last. "The giants didn't live on the beaches."

"You could have mentioned that in the first place," Finn grumbled, but under his breath as Beth was close again.

"Shall we head back?" she asked. "I'm not sure what the tide's doing, and we don't want to be stuck here."

"I… er… I wanted to see the cliff," said Finn. "But you go. I won't be long. And if I get cut off, I'll walk along the cliff path. The guidebook said it isn't far."

"Oo, that sounds fun. I'll come with you."

Finn frowned openly at her.

"I really think you should go back now," he said. "You can tell my parents so they won't get worried."

"I'll send them a text," she said, pulling out a phone he didn't know she possessed. He wasn't one for technology, and right then he hated it more than usual.

"There. Done," she beamed at him.

"Great," said Finn stonily.

The walk up the cliff path was even tougher than scrambling over the rocks had been. Steep didn't do the incline justice, and Finn was panting by the time they reached the top. How high they'd climbed became apparent when he straightened and took in the view. The sea foamed far below, the people foolishly splashing in its waves no more than dots. Despite being a calm day, the wind whipped his face. The fence that had run alongside the track the whole way up had come to a dramatic stop. Without it, the drop became stomach churning. Beth, however, seemingly unconcerned by the possibility of falling to her death, wandered over to the crumbling edge and peered down.

"Wow," she said. "We're on the top of the world!"

Finn subconsciously took a step backwards. "You shouldn't stand so close," he cautioned.

Beth laughed, but obligingly wandered back to him.

Remembering he had a task to complete, Finn scanned his surroundings. As impressive as the view was, the clifftop itself was rather bland. Tufty grass, rough pathways, the odd pile of boulders… certainly nothing that screamed '*Giant's Treasure Trove*'. He considered the two routes that lay before them. They both appeared to continue in the same direction, but one ran alarmingly close to the drop. The other was a smidge more inland.

"Let's go this way," he said, turning pointedly towards the path furthest from the edge.

Without waiting to see who followed, he walked on. The ground was littered with stones, and he winced as they jabbed him through his thin beach shoes, tripping over at times for good measure. Norm bounded ahead, unperturbed by the terrain, and Tomkin practically flew, winding his own route, pouncing on unsuspecting creatures.

"Now *this* reminds me of home," he shouted. "Wild. I love it!"

As Finn tripped for a third time, he made a mental note

never to visit Bodmin Moor. He wasn't sure his ankles could take it.

A great mound of earth and boulders lay on his left, and both Norm and Tomkin headed towards it. Despite not particularly wanting to get any higher, Finn followed them, hoping the vantage would help him spot something, anything, of use.

Scrambling up a dirt track that slipped beneath his feet, he ended up on his knees more than once. To his annoyance, Beth strode effortlessly up a parallel path as if floating.

Once at the top, Finn was disappointed to take in his surroundings. Apart from a few houses inland, and the silhouettes of a couple of engine houses, there wasn't much more to see than lower down.

Exhausted from the climb, he slumped onto a pile of stones, picking a patch slightly softened by a patch of grass.

Beth continued to scrabble over the rocks, following Tomkin.

"I love your cat," she said, clearly not believing Finn's earlier claim not to know him. "My parents won't let me have one. They say they're too dirty. But you're beautiful, aren't you?"

"I like her," called Tomkin, "even if she does speak to me in that stupid voice some humans think animals like."

"You can live with her then," snapped Finn, entirely forgetting about Beth for a second.

"What did you say?" she asked.

"Oh, I was just talking to myself."

Tomkin stuck his tongue out, and Norm laughed.

Finn scowled, scuffing his beach shoes angrily in the dirt, muttering complaints to himself. The brown dust stuck to the patches of wetness on them from where he'd splashed through rock pools. The earth was bone dry, the summer sun having sucked it of all moisture. A peaceful silence descended, and it occurred to him his waking hours had been sorely lacking silence since Norm came into his life. As if on cue, the knocker appeared beside him.

"Watcha doing?" he asked, peering at Finn and destroying his moment of quiet grumpiness.

"Nothing," Finn sighed, pushing to his feet. "Come on, let's get this pointless search over with."

He turned to walk down the mound, glancing behind him to check whether Tomkin and Beth had heard him. The cat was lazily making his way towards them, but Beth was nowhere to be seen.

"Beth?" he called, expecting her to pop up from behind a rock.

Nothing.

"Beth, come on!"

Still nothing.

If she was playing a joke on them, he would not be amused.

"Did you see where she went?" he asked Norm.

"No," replied Norm, shaking his head.

"Tomkin?"

"What?" The cat jumped up next to Finn, a dead mouse dangling from his jaws.

"Eurgh!" cried Finn.

"It's lunchtime," Tomkin defended himself, placing the mouse carefully in front of him. "Now, what were you saying?"

"Where's Beth?"

"No idea. Why? Where is she?"

"That's what I'm asking you!"

Finn was getting more and more worked up, panic overtaking his previous exasperation. He was *sure* she hadn't wandered off towards the cliff edge, but…

"Just help me look, you two," he ordered.

Hurrying over the stones, he quickly realised there was

nowhere for her to hide.

"You don't think she went on?" suggested Norm, looking ahead. "Or fell down a mine?"

"What?" yelped Finn, glancing at the dilapidated remains of mining buildings spread out around them. "They'd cover the openings up, wouldn't they?"

"Maybe," replied Norm, starting to investigate the ground.

Finn joined him, pushing aside rocks as if they might be concealing Beth, but there was nothing to see. There weren't any girl-sized holes lying around.

"This is ridiculous," declared Finn, throwing his hands in the air. He kicked a rather large rock in frustration, immediately regretting it.

"Ow!" he howled in pain.

Sitting down, he yanked his shoe off to reveal his big toe, coated in blood. He cringed as he wiped it gingerly on a nearby patch of moss.

"What did you do that for?" asked Norm.

"I didn't do it on purpose!" exclaimed Finn, shoving his foot back into the shoe and stamping it on the ground in frustration. As he did so, the soil gave way beneath it. He stumbled, gasping with shock as his foot disappeared. Yanking it free, he gaped at the opening. Norm was already on his knees, investigating. Finn dropped down to join him, pulling aside the lump of moss he'd smeared with his blood to reveal a… hole? No, a tunnel? Or was it a cave? Finn's spine tingled.

"Ooo," whispered Norm, his voice echoing back to them from the darkness.

"Beth?" called Finn.

There was no reply.

Finn reached down and pushed aside more earth. The hole grew. He leaned forward, trying to catch a glimpse of anything in the blackness below.

"Finn, be care-…"

But Finn didn't hear the rest of Norm's warning, for at the moment the ground under his hands dropped away completely, toppling him forwards. He fell, headfirst, the dark swallowing both him and his scream.

Ten

Bolster

Finn landed on a moist surface, strangely spongy to the touch. As he got to his feet, he could feel the panic rising in his chest, threatening to suffocate him. He swallowed it down, breathing deeply and making himself think. Squinting, he peered up. A small patch of light told him where the entrance was. Norm's worried face appeared, a silhouette against the blue sky.

"What did you do that for?" he asked.

"I didn't do it on purpose!" replied Finn incredulously.

"Well don't move," Norm shouted. "I'll find something to pull you out."

And just like that, he was gone.

Finn waited, trying to keep his fear at bay. His heart was drumming loudly in his eardrums. He counted the beats, letting the distraction calm him. He'd reached 100 when he remembered why he'd been peering into a dank hole in the first place.

"Beth?" he called out gently. Something told him raising his voice wouldn't be a good idea.

There was no reply, so he took a step further into the dark space. The ground was uneven, and he had to work hard not to trip with every step. Whether it was a cave or a tunnel, he still couldn't decide, but it certainly smelt *awful*. Wrinkling his nose, he felt his way forward until he hit something hard. Reaching out, his hands made contact with a soft, wet, wall. He quickly recoiled, shuddering in repulsion. The feel reminded him of the underside of a snail. Kicking experimentally instead, he discovered the solid base of the wall only rose to his knees before it shelved backwards and rose again, all moist and squidgy. Straining his eyes to see in the gloom, he made out a row of yellow rocks, uniform and covered in moss. Then he let out a gasp. Nestled deep within one of the rocks lay a shell. A shell, the size of his palm, with a domed, ridged surface, creamy white all over and somehow seeming to shine even in the darkness. A shell the exact mirror of the one he'd left tucked safely under his pillow that morning.

Unable to believe his luck, Finn quickly attempted to pick it up. It was stuck much tighter than the other had been, but digging his nails under its edge, he was at last able to loosen it slightly. Giving one last, exhausted pull, the shell finally came free. Finn stumbled backwards, narrowly avoiding landing in a heap. Not caring about the torn skin on his fingertips, he studied the shell. It was undamaged, and as perfect as its twin, pulsing slightly with power in his grip. Glancing at the rock he'd freed it from, he saw it had been covering a hole. None the wiser why it had been there, he hurried back to where he hoped Norm would soon return. Before impatience had a chance to develop, however, the ground beneath him trembled. Dread descended. Of course, it couldn't have been that easy.

"Norm!" he shouted. "Quick!"

No bearded face appeared.

Finn yelped as he felt the cave around him move. The walls sucked in, brushing his fingertips as he held his arms out to steady himself. Fresh, clean air was sucked in from the entrance, until the world paused. Then, an almighty huff of rank wind from deep behind Finn blew, hitting him with such a force it propelled him up and out of the hole.

He sailed into the blindingly bright, blissfully clear sky. Yet any relief at his escape was short-lived, as an enormous hand swung towards him, catching him mid-flight.

A stone hand.

The hand of a giant.

The world span as fingers attempted to close around him. Desperately, Finn twisted, somehow evading the vice like grip.

Free!

Finn realised the downside of his win a moment later, when he dropped like a lead weight.

"I'll save you!" he heard Norm scream dramatically before Finn slammed on top of him.

Norm whimpered, and Finn groaned. He had a pickaxe digging into his bottom, and couldn't help but speculate the soft grass to either side of him would have been far better landing spots.

"Get up the pair of you, and RUN," called Tomkin, from a direction Finn couldn't discern. He felt as if he'd been spun in a washing machine, and then everything was spinning. He tilted his gaze upwards, and suddenly found the motivation he needed to move.

A giant towered above him. Its body was a mass of grey boulders, smattered all over with patches of green moss.

A lumpy sphere on top resembled head, and tufts of grass sprouted like hair. Two dark eyes blinked in the sunlight, and a grimace revealed rows of crumbling teeth. A cry threatened to escape from Finn's mouth, but he clamped his jaw shut. Desperately scrambling up he turned and ran. Beside him, Norm and Tomkin were also galloping.

"Why do I never listen to myself?" grumbled Tomkin as he bounded past. "I knew I shouldn't have come, but here I am. Again!"

Stones slipped beneath Finn's shoes, and the path took on a new danger as he careered downwards. Reaching the fenced section, he practically slid the first few feet on his bottom, uncaring at the cuts he was collecting. All his focus was on escaping until a scream stopped him in his tracks. It was a girl's scream, and he had a sinking feeling why it was so filled with fright. Turning, he saw he was right. The giant, fully standing now, held a tiny figure in his right fist. His fingers obscured most of her, but the face poking out of the top was unmistakable.

Beth.

"Girl?" The giant was booming at her. Whatever magic had been preventing Beth from being able to see magical creatures had clearly worn off, and she surveyed the giant in pure horror. A small trail of blood trickled down her forehead, as if she'd banged it hard. "Girl was in Bolster's armpit, tickling with her breath."

"W… w… what?" Beth stammered. "I fell. I'm sorry. I didn't mean to disturb you. I just fell and hit my head. I… I'm sorry."

The fact Beth could string any words together, and not simply continue to scream, impressed Finn immensely. The giant, however, didn't seem to be listening to her.

"Girl make good wife?" he asked instead. "Cook and clean for Bolster?"

"Finn, we have to do something," urged Norm.

"I'm aware of that," Finn snapped back, "but what?!"

Hearing their voices, Beth looked down at them.

"Don't worry, we'll save you!" Norm shouted up.

A whimper escaped Beth's throat as she took him in, waving his pickaxe in the air.

"Stop it, you're frightening her," hissed Finn.

Deflated, Norm lowered his tool. "Sorry. I'd forgotten she's never seen me before."

"How *can* she see you?" demanded Finn.

"The magic only stretches so far," Norm explained. "If a human is forced to see, like when hauled twenty feet in the hair by a crazed giant, the veil is lifted on everything. She'll be able to hear Tomkin now too."

"Lucky her," Finn muttered to himself.

With Beth's attention drawn to them, the giant also turned his head. Finn had no time to move before two black eyes, like lumps of coal, glared down at him. Bolster's lips curled, and a low rumbling growl emanated from somewhere deep within his chest.

"Thief!" he snarled. "Give shell back! Mine!"

"What shell?" Finn replied, tightening his grip on the shell in his hand, hoping it was fully concealed.

"Bolster not stupid. Give. Hole in tooth hurts without it."

"I really don't…" Finn started to lie, but Bolster released a roar in response and the words died before Finn could speak them.

"I'm not sure lying to a giant is a good idea," whispered Norm. "They're known for having quite a temper."

"You don't say!"

"Give. Back." Bolster shouted, clenching his fists in anger.

Beth whimpered in pain.

"Fine, fine," shouted Finn. "You can have it. Here," he held out his arm, "but let her go first. Please?"

Bolster looked from the shell Finn held to Beth, back and forth, as if the decision was too much for his tiny brain.

"Both?" he suggested.

"No!" cried Finn, determined to keep his nerve. As much as he didn't want to return the shell, if it was the only way to save Beth, he'd do it in a heartbeat.

As Bolster struggled with the choice before him, Beth struggled. Somehow, she managed to get one arm free, and she punched at the giant's hand ferociously. Certainly more bravely than Finn would have done.

"Ow!" cried the giant. "Bolster not like small girl. She is not good wife. Maybe he eats her instead?"

"NO!" Finn waved the shell enticingly to regain Bolster's attention. "Just put her down. She wouldn't taste very nice anyway. And you're right, she'd make a terrible wife. She never stops talking. Look, take the shell. Come on."

Bolster looked even more confused, but rubbing the spot Beth had hit him, he peered at Finn.

"Tooth does hurt," he mused.

Then, without warning, he opened his fist and dropped Beth. In the same instant, faster than Finn would have thought possible, he snatched at the shell. Stone fingers rasped against Finn's skin, but he barely noticed as he starred at where Beth had fallen. She lay crumpled, and a breath caught in Finn's throat as he feared the worse. Amazingly, she moved. Wincing, she pushed herself dazedly to her feet.

Finn rushed towards her. Grabbing her arm, he braved a look at Bolster. Thankfully, he was busy fiddling with his mouth, presumably returning the shell to where Finn had ripped it out.

"Come on, run," he hissed at Beth in a whisper.

Finn pulled her towards the path they'd come up but, as they stepped, Bolster sat down with a thud, still struggling with his tooth. The way was barred. Finn turned instead towards St. Agnes. Without wasting time on thinking, he yanked at Beth, relieved to see Norm and Tomkin waiting for him. Then they were all running. Finn didn't glance back, but Norm, managing to sprint and peer over his shoulder at the same time, provided a constant commentary.

"He's looking around."

"He's scratching his head."

"Now he's scratching all over. Gross!"

"Oo, now he's lying down. He's not coming after us!"

Despite the news, Finn didn't slow his pace, not until the path dropped downwards and he feared he'd slip and break his neck. Steps flowed in front of them, and he jumped down them, reaching a gate which read 'Garden Path to the Beach'.

"This way," he called, throwing himself forwards again, and down yet more steps.

When they finally came out onto the road, Finn was panting. People were everywhere, and they were giving him suspicious looks as he bent onto his knees, taking a few deep, rasping breaths. Next to him, Beth was shaking, and it occurred to Finn how weird they must look.

"Try to be normal," he said to Beth as he straightened, plastering a smile onto his face.

Thankfully, she followed his order and even released a little laugh.

"Good race," she said, loudly enough that the frowns of the passers-by relaxed, and she and Finn slipped into the crowd walking to the beach without issue.

They wandered as casually as they could, not saying a word. The sky, so blue when they'd arrived that morning, had grown dark and threatening. Just before they reached the spot where their parents were relaxing, Beth grabbed Finn by the arm, forcing him to stop.

"Finn," she demanded. "What…?" She glanced at Norm. "Who?" She stared at Tomkin. "How?"

Finn opened his mouth, unsure how best to reply, when a roll of thunder echoed through the air. Rain followed within seconds, causing everyone on the beach to squeal and begin hurriedly packing their bags.

"There you two are," called out Finn's mum. "Quick,

come and grab some stuff before everything's soaked through. We'll have to eat our sandwiches in the car!"

Thankful for the distraction, Finn simply shrugged before turning away.

On the walk to the carpark, he stayed next to his parents, avoiding Beth's pointed glances.

"You'll have to talk to her at some point," said Norm. "There's no way you can pretend all that didn't happen. What if she tells someone?"

"Even if she did, who'd believe her?" Finn whispered back. "Of course, my parents would, but they'd never admit it. The only thing Beth would achieve is looking totally barking mad."

"Don't you think we owe her an explanation after everything that's just happened?"

"No," said Finn stubbornly and, if he was honest with himself, unreasonably. "It was *her* decision to stick her nose into our business."

"I doubt she expected to be almost forced into marriage with a stone giant!"

Finn closed his mouth and refused to continue the conversation. He had a bigger issue to work out at that moment, anyway. In the mad rush to leave the beach, with the rain pouring down, he hadn't thought to get Tomkin into his bag. As they approached the car, he realised too late. His parents had flung open the doors, leaping in with armfuls of stuff.

"Get in Finn, it's getting worse," said Mum, frowning at him as he stood there, gormless and glancing from the dripping cat a few metres away to the open car door.

"Er, Mum," he said, scurrying forwards and ducking his head inside the car. "I think that cat must have got in the car earlier as it's... er... it's here."

Mum's expression flashed from concern to stony disapproval.

"What?"

"Look..." He pointed behind him, where Tomkin was glaring.

"Leave it," said Dad coldly. "I seriously doubt it's the same one."

"But look at the size of it. There can't be that many enormous cats who like to follow me around? We can't just leave him here!"

Genuine worry grew in his chest.

"If they make me walk back in the rain," threatened Tomkin, "I am going to poo on their doorstep."

"If it scratches my car, I will dump him by the side of the road, I swear," said Dad.

With the two threats hanging ominously in the air, Finn finally got in, making space for Tomkin at his feet.

"Please be good," he hissed.

"I sort of wish I had fleas to leave everywhere," Tomkin muttered in reply. "Dump me by the side of the road indeed. How dare he!!"

Finn groaned internally and took the limp sandwich passed to him.

"I don't think it'll stop," commented Mum, peering out at the rain.

A conversation with Beth's parents followed, shouted through open windows, and they all agreed to give up and head home.

"Maybe we can come back another day?" Beth called from her seat, smiling at Finn conspiratorially.

He didn't reply.

Eleven

How To Trick A Giant

The next morning, Finn woke tired and grumpy. Memories of the giant had kept him tossing and turning all night, but it was more than that; he felt an immense weight of disappointment. He'd failed. The story of the mermaid might earn him a few moments of glory, but it'd soon die out when he revealed that he'd given up and hadn't actually saved the sea princess after all.

"We can go back?" suggested Norm, correctly picking up on Finn's mood. "There must be a way to convince Bolster to give up the shell."

"Hmph," was Finn's only response.

The rain was still hammering outside, and Mum and Dad had agreed a day in would be a good idea. Finn took that as the perfect excuse to curl up on his bed with his disguised school books. Try as he might, however, he couldn't concentrate, the words of the incantations he was attempting to memorize sliding across the page like butter. Instead, the feel of that second shell in his palm kept returning to him.

Sighing, he pulled the first one out from under his pillow and starred at it. It showed no signs of power, and yet... there was something. Some hint of magic that called to him. He could only imagine what it could do when untied with its pair. Dare he continue and find out?

He attempted to return to his reading once more, but it was no good.

"Fine," he declared, more to himself than anyone else, "we can try again."

Tomkin certainly wasn't listening and didn't even twitch an ear as he slept at the foot of the bed.

Norm, however, at least grunted a *What?* from the floor where he was...

"What *are* you doing?" Finn quizzed, noticing for the first time that Norm was surrounded by cushions.

"Making a den," explained Norm, his voice muffled as

he retreated inside the dark space he created. "I miss being underground."

"Oh, ok," said Finn, unable to conjure any other response. "But, if you're done, could you help me now? I've decided to keep going."

"I knew you weren't a coward," whooped Norm.

"And *I* knew you weren't as clever as you claimed," piped up Tomkin at last.

Finn's first action, as always when faced with a problem, was to turn to books. The cottage they were renting was well stocked with them, and most were related to Cornwall. He found a slim edition titled *The Myths and Legends of Cornwall*, and settled down on his bed to see if it had anything about giants that could prove useful. To his surprise, the story of Bolster had earned itself a whole chapter, but his hope soon fell.

"This is useless," he grumbled.

"Why?" asked Norm. He'd grabbed a stack of books too, but rather than read them, he was using them to build a porch on his den.

"Everything they claim in here is clearly nonsense," said Finn.

"How do you know?" quizzed Norm.

"It ends with Bolster bleeding to death and staining the cliffs red with his blood."

"So?"

Finn looked at him in disbelief.

"Er, was it only me that saw him yesterday? Moving, shouting, ALIVE!" Finn snorted. "Either we saw a ghost, or this book's account that Agnes' trick killed Bolster is a massive lie."

"Ah, but it's almost impossible to kill a giant. It's more likely they rendered him unconscious and simply believed him to be dead. Giants can sort of go into hibernation mode like that. It doesn't mean the rest of the story is a lie."

"Even if it's not, I don't see how it can help us."

"Humans are rather stupid, aren't they?" said Tomkin to Norm, joining the conversation half way through as he so often did. "He makes you seem like a genius at times."

"Look, I'm tired ok?" argued Finn. "I'm actually really smart."

"Then use that brain of yours. You're faced with a giant who has what you want, but he's a giant that's susceptible to being tricked. Add to that the fact you know *exactly* what he likes, and I'd say the plan is quite obvious."

Finn thought for a second, running through what Tomkin had said. What was it that Bolster liked? He didn't dare ask for fear of being ridiculed again.

Just then, he heard a knock on the front door. A moment later, Mum's voice called up the stairs.

"Finn, Beth is here to see you."

Finn gasped as the mention of Beth made the cogs in his brain click.

"Bolster wants a wife!"

"Bingo!"

Before he could say anymore, Finn heard footsteps approaching

"Hide," he hissed.

Both Norm and Tomkin tried to protest, but Finn shoved them forcibly into the wardrobe without listening, earning himself a little nip from Tomkin. He was sucking the wound on his finger when Mum pushed open his door without knocking. Letting Beth in, she closed them all in together without another word.

Finn stood in silence as Beth scanned the room, eyes narrowing.

"So, are you going to tell me what's going on?" she said, her focus finally returning to Finn.

"What do you mean?" Finn squeaked, putting his hand on his hip in what he hoped was a casual manner.

It wasn't, and Beth raised a single eyebrow at him.

"Finn, do you think I'm an idiot? Yesterday, the cliffs turned into a giant that threatened to eat me, and I heard your cat talk. Not to mention that weird little garden gnome that was running about all over the place."

"Oi," shouted Norm, jumping out of the wardrobe at the insult. "Who are you calling a garden gnome?! I'll have you know I am a knocker. Gnome?! I ask you!"

"Forgive him, he's under the illusion that knocker is better than a gnome," purred Tomkin, appearing from behind Norm.

Finn threw his arms up in exasperation.

To Beth's credit, she didn't scream at the sudden arrivals, although her eyes went rather wide.

"But why does everyone keep thinking I'm a gnome?" cried Norm, his anger being replaced by despair. "Is it the beard? Shall I shave it off?"

"It's not the beard," said Beth, surprising Finn further by engaging with Norm. She studied him thoughtfully. "It's…"

"His general gnominess?" suggested Tomkin helpfully.

Norm stuck out his bottom lip, sulking as the others laughed.

"I think gnomes are amazing," said Beth kindly, tucking a stray strand of auburn hair behind her ear and bending closer to him. "But please tell me what you are?"

Norm puffed up his chest and bowed. "I am a Cornish knocker," he announced.

Beth shook his hand politely. "Pleased to meet you."

"I like this one," said Norm. "Maybe I should switch children. I don't suppose you're a wizard too?" Norm sniffed her.

"No," she replied. Why she didn't flee at Norm's sniffing, Finn did not know. Instead, she turned to scrutinise him. "Is that what you are then?"

He sighed resignedly.

"Yes, but it's nothing to worry about," he said. "Just don't tell anyone. In fact, when I get back to school, I'll tell my teachers and they'll sort it you get your memory altered. You won't have to live your life freaked out, like my parents," he added wistfully under his breath. "So now you know, you can leave us alone and get on with your own holiday."

"Finn!" chided Norm.

"Anyway," added Tomkin. "You need her, don't you think?"

Finn couldn't meet the challenge in Tomkin's eyes.

"Fine!" he cried in defeat. "I guess I have to tell you what's going on."

So he did. It didn't take as long as he expected, even with Norm interrupting every two seconds to add some pointless extra piece of information.

"You can run away now," said Finn when he'd finished. "Feel free to call me a weirdo as you go."

"I don't think you're a weirdo," replied Beth. "I think it's all rather cool."

"Really?" said Finn, mildly surprised at her acceptance of all the strangeness.

"What I still don't understand, though, is why you need me?"

Finn paused, not wanting to include her any further, but his brain wouldn't provide a better plan. He swallowed his annoyance.

"It's to do with Bolster, and how to convince him to give me the shell."

Beth simply waited for him to go on.

"We think he'd give it to us in return for you."

"But…" stammered Beth, the first signs of alarm flashing across her face. "But… if you wanted to sacrifice me for the shell, why didn't you do it yesterday? Why did you bother saving me?"

"I don't mean we should let him keep you!" cried Finn, horrified. "I'm not an evil wizard."

"Oh… well… good, because I thought that would be quite awful of you."

"No, I was planning on tricking him."

"How?"

"I… I hadn't worked that bit out yet."

"Oh," she repeated. "Ok then, let me help."

"Seriously? You want to help us? Even if it involves using you as bait?" Finn was becoming begrudgingly impressed by this freckled girl.

Beth shrugged. "It's more interesting than playing on the beach on my own."

"I suppose that's true." Finn felt suddenly very guilty for how mean he'd been to her. "Thanks," he added, offering her a small smile.

Her own tooth-gapped grin beamed back at him in return and, just like that, they became friends.

Before Beth settled down, she insisted she needed to gather some 'important supplies' first. She dashed off, leaving a puzzled Finn questioning whether he'd done the right thing to include her.

When she returned, her arms were full with piles of books, notepads and various items of stationary, which she spread out neatly on his desk. Finn edged to take a closer look as she unzipped a bag and lined up pencils, post-it notes and highlighters.

"You're a geek!" he gasped, but not in horror. He was delighted.

Beth scowled before she noticed the expression of wonder on Finn's face as he reached to inspect her page dividers.

"I'm just organised," she corrected. "And... well, research is fun. I doubt any of these books will be very useful, they're just the ones I could find in our cottage on Cornish folklore. This, however, should help." She held up a bright orange case that held some sort of electronic tablet.

Finn grimaced. "I'm not into technology." he said. "Wizards don't use it at all."

"Seriously? But it's so amazing. I bet it holds the key."

"I'll stick to the books," he said dismissively, picking up the whole pile and carrying them it over to his bed, rather destroying Norm's den in the process.

The knocker didn't notice, however, as he was busy clambering up next to Beth to get a closer look at her tablet. He then asked her a million questions about her tablet, gasping distractingly loudly every 30 seconds.

They spent the rest of the morning trying, and failing, to come up with a decent plan. The rain from the day before continued to hammer down, so they were at least uninterrupted by adults, apart from the frequent offering of snacks from Mum and Dad. Finn was never normally fed so regularly, so he could only guess it was their way of spying on him. Finn could only be thankful, however, for at least when Norm had food in his mouth he was quiet for a few seconds. Long periods of focused concentration were clearly not his strength, and he yo-yoed between Finn and Beth, asking pointless questions and wondering out loud if it was almost lunchtime yet. When Dad actually did appear carrying a massive tray and announcing "lunch had arrived", Finn was more than ready to take a break. As he, Norm and Tomkin crowded around the tray, Beth remained where she sat, muttering to herself.

"I'd seriously take what you want before Norm inhales everything," Finn warned her, but she waved him away and continued to read, scribbling notes on a pad of paper as she went.

"Suit yourself," he said before grabbing a bag of crisps from beneath Norm's outstretched hand and adding it to his plate.

He had barely bitten into his second sandwich, shielding it protectively from Norm, who'd already eaten five and was eyeing Finn's with desire, when Beth slammed down her pencil triumphantly.

"I might have found something," she announced.

"What, on that thing?" Finn asked, wrinkling his nose but putting his sandwich down in surprise.

"It's got the internet on it, Finn," she explained. "It literally holds all the information in the world."

"Humph," he huffed, scowling at the pile of books that had failed him. He reached to pick up his sandwich again, but his fingers closed on thin air. There was nothing but crumbs left on his plate.

"So what did you find?" said Norm, struggling to talk with his mouth stuffed full.

"Oi, you stole my sandwich," cried Finn.

"I don't know what you're talking about," declared Norm, his eyes wide and innocent, even as flecks of half chewed bread sprayed from his mouth.

"You really should have let me eat him when I first arrived," said Tomkin. "It would have saved you a lot of bother."

"Does anyone want to hear what I've found out?" interrupted Beth.

"Yes, fine, what has the mighty *internet* got to say about how we can outsmart a vicious giant?" grumbled Finn.

"Well, I was looking up tales about giants, and the way people have beat them in the past," explained Beth, "and I found a load of stories about a tailor who did these tricks on them. I reckon one of them might be perfect to use on Bolster."

"What were they?" asked Finn, intrigued despite himself.

"They're mainly tests of strength," said Beth, "but with the tailor using cunning to win. I thought you could challenge Bolster. Say you're stronger than he is? Bet him you can prove it, with the winner getting both me and the shell?"

"How on earth can I beat him in a test of strength? That's impossible."

"That's where the tricks come in," said Beth. "Weren't you listening?"

"Yeah Finn," said Norm. "The sailor's got tricks. I thought you said you were clever?"

"It's tailor, not sailor," growled Finn through gritted teeth, still bitter about his sandwich.

"What's a tailor?"

"Someone who sews clothes," explained Beth, "but that's not important. Listen to what he did." She picked up her notebook and scanned her notes. "Firstly, he told the giant he faced that he was *so* strong, he could squeeze water out of a stone."

"Well that's ridiculous," interrupted Finn rudely.

"The giant tried," Beth continued, ignoring him, "but crumbled his rock to dust. Then it was the tailor's turn."

"What happened?" gasped Norm, gripping the edge of Finn's bed in anticipation.

"He squeezed with all his might, and water dripped out, but it wasn't a rock that he held. It was this wet cheese, so easy to get water out of. Anyway, the giant was fooled, and the tailor won!"

"You want me to pretend cheese is a rock and squeeze it until it drips?" asked Finn stonily.

"Seriously? That's the worst plan I've ever heard."

"I don't know," Norm chimed, "I think it's brie-liant. Get it? Get it?"

Finn winced.

"That joke stinks," said Tomkin.

"What, like cheese?" Norm retorted, doubling over with glee.

Beth watched him, bewilderment etched all over her face.

"Try to ignore him," suggested Tomkin. "Life becomes far easier when you do."

"Or cheesier!" Norm shouted, his laughter having overtaken him so strongly tears of mirth were trickling down his cheeks and into his beard.

Beth opened and closed her mouth a few times before managing to take Tomkin's advice and turn back to Finn.

"It's just a starting point," she explained. "Here, listen to what happened next. When the giant demanded another test, they had a throwing competition. The giant's stone obviously travelled miles before it landed, but the tailor threw a bird, pretending it was a stone. It flew away and never landed. So he won again."

"No way," cried Finn. "I am *not* throwing a bird!"

"Are you sure?" asked Tomkin. "I'd happily catch one for you?"

"No!"

Tomkin sighed in disappointment. "Spoilsport."

"Any other bright ideas?" Finn asked Beth.

"Not really," she admitted. "The tailor did other stuff, but it all gets a bit far-fetched."

"More far-fetched than squeezing cheese or throwing defenceless animals into the air?!"

"Ok, ok, I agree that bird throwing is a bit much, but the cheese thing could work."

"How? I mean, what sort of cheese can you even squeeze water from?"

"I don't know, I'm not a cheese expert!"

Norm, who'd finally stopped giggling enough to pick

himself up off the floor, opened his mouth with a grin.

"I swear," warned Finn menacingly, "if you make one more cheese joke, I'll put you outside and won't feed you for a week."

Norm's eyebrows shot upwards and he shut his lips, pouting slightly.

Finn reached forward and snatched a tomato from the bowl of salad Mum had provided with lunch, the only thing Norm hadn't touched. He bit into it, and a spray of juice spurted out and dribbled down his t-shirt.

"Eurgh," he complained whilst Norm chuckled.

Beth, however, studied him strangely.

"Why are you looking at me like that?" asked Finn, self-consciously wiping the juice from his chin. "Do I have pips on my face?"

"I've got to go," was all Beth said in response. "Wait here."

Not touching her piles of stuff, she dashed out of the room. Then, Finn heard the front door slam.

"Are all girls that weird?" he gaped at Norm and Tomkin.

"Some are worse," confirmed Norm.

Finn shook his head in disbelief. "I'm not sure letting her join us was a good idea."

"Oh, I don't know," yawned Tomkin. "She's

entertainingly bonkers, in an irritating sort of way."

Finn continued to wonder about the mystery of girls, yet apart from flicking aimlessly through his books, he had little to do but wait and hope Beth returned with a plan. When she bounded back up the stairs, less than ten minutes later, her face was flush with excitement as she held out a round, orange object, practically throwing it at Finn.

"What about this?" she said.

Finn frowned at the thing in his hands. "An orange?"

Norm approached, sniffing. "Looks delicious," he said.

"It's not to eat," chastised Beth, and Norm hung his head in disappointment. "And it's not an ordinary orange, it's a blood orange. My dad eats one for breakfast every morning, says it's good for his immune system or something."

"And… what? We should get a bag of these and throw them at Bolster until he gives us the shell?"

"That sounds fun," said Norm, "but I don't think it'd work, giants are very tough. I vote we eat them instead." His little hand reached out for the fruit again.

"Norm!" snapped Finn. "If I promise to get you another packet of biscuits in a minute, will you sit still and be quiet?!"

Norm's face lit up with delight and he mimed zipping his mouth shut.

Sighing with relief, Finn turned back to Beth.

"Just explain," he pleaded. "And *please* do it before he starts jabbering or my head might explode."

"Ok," said Beth, sitting back on the desk chair. "I think I've got a way for you to challenge Bolster to a test of strength, and win."

Finn raised his eyebrows doubtfully.

"This should be interesting," snorted Tomkin.

Beth explained her plan. When she was finished, she was met with three unconvinced stares.

Finn closed his eyes and shook his head, realising it was instances like these that made him prefer working alone. Other people were stupid. Or crazy. Or, in this case, both.

"Tomkin, Norm," he said. "Please tell her this is a ridiculous idea?"

"You're aware I consider all plans that don't involve sleeping in a comfy spot terrible," said Tomkin, "so I'm not sure she'll consider my opinion valid."

"Norm?" beseeched Finn, but when he turned, he realised the knocker was busy stuffing all the remaining tomatoes in his mouth, and not listening to a word.

With a gulp, Norm swallowed.

"You made them look tasty," he said, "so I wanted to

give them a go. What were you saying?"

"Forget it," said Finn. "You've not proved yourself intelligent enough to get a vote. You should hang out with Bolster some time, you two are probably be on the same wavelength, you'd get on perfectly!"

"Come on," cajoled Beth. "It really could work, I know it could. I wouldn't be willing to risk my own safety otherwise."

Finn knew she had a point, that it was her that would be in danger if things went wrong.

"Fine," he agreed at last.

Beth cheered.

Finn groaned.

Tomkin rolled his eyes.

Norm searched the lunch tray for any last scraps of food.

"It's going to be great," Beth promised. "But, to trick a giant, even one as stupid as Bolster, you'll have to play the part. Be so full of yourself he'll actually believe you *could* be strong."

"Well," huffed Finn, "luckily for us, we have the Master of Arrogance at our disposal to teach me his ways."

"Did somebody say my name?" purred Tomkin.

Twelve

A Contest Of Strength

As it turned out, coming up with the plan wasn't half as difficult as convincing both sets of their parents to return to St. Agnes.

"But we've seen it now," said Mrs Burnett. "Don't you kids fancy trying somewhere new? I've heard very good things about the amusement park in Helston. It's got historical experiences as well as rides," she added, addressing Finn directly.

He grimaced internally.

"No Mum," said Beth, saving Finn from having to answer. "We really liked climbing over the rocks, and the cliffs were cool too. There's so much still to explore."

The adults all shared a look. They'd been suggesting other options for the best part of twenty minutes, and Finn and Beth had remained resolute in their refusals.

"Fine," they all agreed at last.

Thankfully, the following day dawned bright and clear. Finn hadn't fancied trying to outwit a giant on a cliff in gale force winds. As they clambered up the winding steps, Tomkin stalked ahead. He was sulking. He hadn't wanted to come at all, but a reminder of what he owed Norm, and a promise from Beth to share her tuna sandwich, had him climb into Finn's bag. It was grudgingly, though, and he had barely spoken a word to any of them since. Finn wished the same could be said for Norm.

"Are you sure this is going to work?" he asked as they reached the top of the cliff, making the climb up from St. Agnes this time, Finn having decided it was preferable to clambering across the beach.

"Why would you say that now? You wouldn't shut up yesterday about how brilliant you thought this plan was!"

"Yes, but, you know, now we're here it's all a bit scarier isn't it?"

"Stop worrying so much," interrupted Beth. "It'll be

fine. I'm the one on offer, remember? If I'm happy, then surely *you* lot should be?"

Despite her words, Finn wasn't sure she *looked* entirely happy. Her usually rosy face was pale, and she chewed on a nail whenever she wasn't speaking. Still, the smile she gave had him shrugging off his concerns.

Norm was studying Beth too, but with a sympathetic expression. "The trouble is," he said, "your confidence could be insanity. It's very common in humans. Many don't realise how mad they are. It's quite sad."

"You better not get eaten," grumbled Tomkin. "I want my promised sandwich,"

"Can you all stop it?" pleaded Finn. "Let's get this over and done with. If I do have to be eaten by an angry giant, I'd rather do it before I get hungry myself."

"It's me he'll eat," said Beth.

"For some reason, I don't believe he'll contain his eating to just you if he works out we tricked him."

"Good point," agreed Beth. "Although, on the plus side, if he eats all of us no one has to deal with explaining what happened to our parents. That would be a tough conversation!"

"You really are worryingly optimistic," commented Tomkin as Finn's eyes went wide with horror.

"It's the madness," whispered Norm.

"You're all mad," muttered Finn, but they weren't listening to him.

When they reached the spot Bolster had appeared, it was impossible to tell that the ground had transformed into a living beast only two days before. The uneven piles of rock and dirt looked like they'd been there forever, and Finn started to doubt they were in the right place.

"Is this definitely it?" he said. "We passed another mound a moment ago, what if that was him?"

"No," said Beth, looking around, "that was too far along. We'd only just got to the top at this end."

Finn knew she was right, but still studied the mound intently. Now they were there, the thought of actually making Bolster appear felt ridiculous. If the others felt the same, however, they weren't showing it. Beth and Norm were collecting handfuls of stones, and Tomkin had retreated a few feet, stretching out in the grass.

"This should be a pleasant spot to watch from," he said.

"Are you seriously not going to help at all?" asked Finn.

"From what I remember, I didn't have a distinct role in the plan," he said, "so I've allocated myself the title of spectator. I think it suits me rather well."

Finn rolled his eyes, but hurried to grab some rocks too, as Norm and Beth had already started throwing theirs at the mound they all hoped was the sleeping giant. They'd decided that this was the best way to try to rouse Bolster, assuming it was the physical pain of having the shell ripped from his tooth that had stirred him previously.

Chucking his first stone, Finn winced at the impact. One thing they didn't want was a Bolster so angry he gobbled them all up before they'd even made him an offer.

After they'd thrown a dozen stones each, they'd all given up attempting to be gentle.

"Why won't the lazy brute wake up?" exclaimed Beth, flinging rocks with a force that sent shingles spraying where they landed.

"We must be doing something wrong," replied Finn. He paused and thought. "What happened last time?" he asked Beth. "What happened to you?"

"I slipped down a hole, apparently into his armpit," Beth shuddered, "and knocked myself unconscious. When I woke up, the ground was moving and, well... you were there for the rest."

"Hmm," mused Finn.

"Maybe he's ticklish?" suggested Norm. "Maybe his

armpit is the key? Does anyone have a feather?"

"I'm not voluntarily going anywhere near that armpit again," protested Beth.

"Anyway," interrupted Finn before Norm could continue. "That can't be it, as Bolster didn't wake until after that."

"Go through everything else that happened. Exactly," ordered Beth.

"We were looking for you," Finn remembered, "but couldn't see anywhere you could have gone. No holes or anything. Then I cut my foot, and I was just sitting down to inspect yet another holiday injury when I found this... opening."

Finn's stomach churned at the knowledge that it had actually been Bolster's mouth.

"You cut yourself?" asked Beth, her attention snagging on the detail, looking thoughtful.

"So?"

"Oo," said Norm, excitedly glancing from Finn's foot to Beth. "That could be it!"

"What?" frowned Finn, hating that even *Norm* had worked it out quicker than him.

"Magical blood," replied Norm. "What if it was the power in your blood that woke him?"

Finn considered that for a second. For once, Norm was making sense.

"Cut yourself and rub a bit of blood about, see if it does anything?" suggested Norm, ruining any faith Finn had in him. "You can borrow my axe if you want?"

"No!" cried Finn.

"It's worth a go, surely?" said Beth.

"Seriously?"

They stared at him expectantly. Even Tomkin wasn't howling at the ridiculousness of Norm's idea.

"Just to be clear, you want me to rub my blood on the earth to wake a sleeping giant?"

They all nodded.

"Fine, fine." Finn threw his hands in the air in defeat. "You're all bonkers, but who am I to argue? I am not, however, using that," he insisted, as Norm held out his axe.

"I can scratch you if you like?" offered Tomkin.

Finn merely scowled at him as he sat down and pulled off his sandal. A plaster hid the cut from before, but the scab was easy to pick at once exposed. A tiny speck of red welled, and Finn caught in on his finger before rubbing it on a stone that he hoped formed part of Bolster. Immediately, Norm and Beth threw yet another collection of stones. This time, it only took a couple of hits before the earth beneath their feet trembled.

"Stand back!" cried Finn, yanking his sandal on before scrambling out of the way. Unfortunately, this involved moving closer to the unfenced cliff edge. Gulping, Finn turned from the drop as the form of Bolster emerged upwards.

"Who wakes Bolster?" howled his gravelly voice. "Not nice. I was dreaming of eating seagulls. Not wanted to be woken. Angry now."

"Er, you know how I asked if this was a good idea?" said Norm, his voice squeaky with fear. "Maybe we should go away and discuss it a little more?"

"Finn, you're up," instructed Beth, giving him a little push.

Finn tried not to tremble as he squared his shoulders and looked up at Bolster.

"Bolster!" he yelled before the giant could gather himself enough to eat them without giving them a chance to speak. He tried to make him sound self-assured, like Tomkin had told him. "I have returned to demand you give me the shell you possess, for I am Finn the Mighty, and you should tremble before me."

Finn cringed at the words, but Beth nodded at him encouragingly and Norm gave him a thumbs up. Tomkin rolled on his tuft of grass in a fit of laughter, but Finn couldn't worry about him, not when Bolster was bending forwards, examining him.

"You don't look very mighty," he said, squinting at Finn and pursing his lips. "Small? Yes. Scrawny? Definitely! Bolster thinks you picked the wrong name."

"I *am* mighty. In fact, Bolster, I declare I am even stronger that *you*!"

Bolster's laughter started as a small rumble, but, as his mirth grew, the whole cliff shook.

"You? You? Stronger than Bolster?! Tiny human is crazy."

"I am not crazy," Finn shouted to be heard over the giant's guffaw. "And I will prove it to you. Let's have a challenge of strength? A duel to determine which of us is truly the mightiest?"

Bolster tilted his head as he considered Finn's offer.

"What duel?"

Finn paused before he answered. This moment, Beth had told him, was key. He couldn't allow Bolster to guess that the duel had been planned. He pretended to look around, as if searching for an idea.

"These stones," he said at last. "I declare I am *so strong*, that I can squeeze blood from them."

Bolster went very quiet. Finn could almost see the cogs of his brain turning as he tried to understand Finn's statement.

"Explain," he demanded at last.

"The earth here was once soaked with your blood. Only someone of immense strength could squeeze it out again. Whichever one of us makes it drip first, is the winner."

"Winner of what?"

"The winner of glory, the shell and…" Finn faltered, but Beth gave him a determined nod. "And," he forced himself to say, "her."

Finn pointed, and Bolster was silent as he fixed his black eyes on Beth.

"So," he said at last, painfully slowly as if the cogs of his brain where struggling to process the information presented to him, "all Bolster must do to keep shell and get new wife, is be stronger than puny human?"

"Yes. Whoever gets blood out of their stone first," confirmed Finn, purposely repeating the terms clearly, "wins the shell and the… girl." He grimaced apologetically at Beth, but her gaze was on Bolster, waiting for his response.

"Deal," the giant thundered.

"Deal," echoed Finn.

Beth clapped in delight, though her hands shook slightly

as Bolster grinned down at her.

"Gentlemen," Norm announced, stepping forward and apparently adopting the role of commentator, "select your rocks."

Finn made a good show of examining the stones at his feet. He weighted some in his hands before discarding them, biding his time before he picked up the orange Beth had placed on ground when they'd arrived. He checked it theatrically before nodding to himself, his sweaty palms causing patches of paint to stick to his fingertips. Hastily he wiped his palms on his shorts before returning his attention to Bolster. The rock the giant had selected was roughly the same size as Finn. He wanted to step backward as he imagined Bolter dropping it on his head and squashing him flat.

"Are you ready?" called Norm. Excitement tinged his words, and Finn could tell he'd got carried away and was enjoying himself far too much.

"Prepare to squeeze in 3... 2... 1... GO!" Norm jumped in the air, his squealing cry so piercing that Finn winced.

Then, before he could attack the painted piece of fruit he held, dust fell from above. Glancing up, the source was immediately visible. Bolster had not wasted a second and was attacking his boulder with a ferocity that had Finn cringing.

"Finn," hissed Beth. "Come on!"

At once, Finn snapped out of his daze, suddenly fearing that Bolster would somehow achieve the impossible. Anxiety drove him to smash the blood orange harder than he thought he was capable of. Liquid instantly squirted from the pre-prepared holes Beth had made earlier with a fork. It dribbled down his forearms, surprisingly blood-like, gleaming in the midday sun.

"We have a winner," screamed Norm, spinning in circles until he fell over from the dizziness.

Bolster looked at his rock, as if expecting to see blood, fully believing it was him being declared the winner. When he saw only rubble, and then noticed the red wetness coating Finn, he released a below of rage that extinguished all Finn's delight in an instance. He clasped Beth's arm as he watched the giant stand completely upright, towering over them.

"Not fair," he roared to the sky, throwing his head back. "Me wants shell and wife. Boy can't have beaten Bolster!"

"But he did," stated Beth. "He won, fair and square, so now you have to give us the shell."

How Beth could keep a straight face as she claimed all was fair, Finn didn't know, but then it wasn't *her* dripping in sticky orange juice. He hoped Bolster's sense of smell was as dim as the rest of him.

Angrily, Bolster thrust his hand into his mouth and, after poking about for a moment, pulled out the shell. It dripped with saliva, but shone enticingly. Finn fixed his gaze upon it.

Bolster's hand reached down, but then he paused. His enormous eyes roved around, scanning the clifftop, inspecting the surrounding area.

"No one here," Finn heard him mutter to himself. "No one saw Bolster lose. Maybe it didn't happen?"

"Er, what?!" stammered Finn.

"Maybe tiny humans are wrong," he continued, ignoring Finn entirely. "Maybe Bolster won and gets his prize?"

"I don't like the sound of this," said Norm.

Tomkin was backing away, hissing softly.

"I think we should run," whispered Beth.

"But the shell. He owes us the shell!" Finn was feeling indignant. The fact they'd tricked Bolster wasn't relevant to him right then. All he could focus on was that the giant was being such a sore loser. "He lost, he has to give it to us!"

"Er, I don't think he sees it that way," said Norm, who was now pulling on Finn's sleeve, attempting to get him back onto the path whilst Bolter was still talking to himself.

Reluctantly, Finn allowed himself to be led, but he hadn't taken more than a couple of steps when Bolster's

149

attention snapped back to them.

"My new wife," he cried, beaming down at Beth. "I'm so glad to have won you back."

"Are you crazy?" shouted Beth. "You lost."

"Now, now," crooned Bolster. "New wife must be nice to Bolster. Otherwise Bolster will eat her, remember?"

As he spoke, he reached down, his monstrous fist reaching towards Beth up. Finn pushed her behind him and Norm leapt forward, brandishing his pickaxe. Beth, however, let out an almighty scream, so loud and piercing Bolster halted and clutched his hands to his ears. They had no time to make the most of Bolster's momentary pause, however, as a rumble rippled beneath them.

"New wife very noisy," Bolster complained with a groan. "Now you've woken her up."

Thirteen

The Other Wife

"Look!" shouted Norm. Finn didn't need to ask at what. To their right, along the clifftop, the earth was moving. The mound they'd passed on their way was sitting up, stretching and forming an all too familiar shape.

"Not another one," groaned Finn.

"Well, I didn't see that coming," said Tomkin.

"What do we do? What do we do?" Norm had started to panic, pulling on his beard anxiously.

Finn had no answer. He was too busy gasping at the new giant, whom was slowly turning in their direction.

"It's a woman," said Beth, somewhat to Finn's surprise.

He had no idea how she could tell and was at a loss to see why it mattered.

"You!" growled the new giant. Its voice was deep, but a pitch higher than Bolster's. "You ugly lump," she went on, "what have you been up to now?"

She was speaking to Bolster, who looked horrified at the addition to their gathering.

"Er... um..." he stammered in response. He attempted to move and place himself in front of Beth, but it was no use.

"Who are they?" the female giant asked sharply. Her gaze found Beth. "Who is *she*?" she repeated more pointedly. "You haven't been trying to replace me with a new wife again, have you?"

"She's his wife!" cried Finn, Beth and Norm together.

"This twist just gets better and better," said Tomkin, slinking to stand beside Finn.

Bolster hadn't replied, but his guilt radiated off him in waves.

"How dare you!" screeched Mrs Bolster. "You useless, ungrateful boulder."

In a flash, Mrs Bolster grabbed a stone from next to her and threw it at her husband. It hit him squarely on the head. The crack of the impact echoed through the air. So did Bolster's howl of pain. Mrs Bolster didn't stop there, however.

The insults and rocks continued to fly. Bolster's hands flew out to protect himself. As they did, the shell dropped from them, falling to the ground unnoticed by everyone but Finn.

"As entertaining as this is," said Tomkin, shouting to be heard over the din, "can I suggest we leave before we all get squashed?"

"Go, I'll catch you up," said Finn.

He dashed forwards. The ground was uneven and shaking so much he struggled to stay upright. Splinters of sharp rock flew everywhere, threatening to slice at his skin. Only the sight of the small, white shell kept him moving.

At last he reached it. Snatching it up he turned to run, thrusting it in his pocket. There was no sign of the others, so he could only hope they were already on their way to safety. Though where they'd gone, Finn couldn't be sure. Pausing for a fraction of a second, he looked in the direction they'd come, the one that led to Mrs Bolster, still screaming and throwing rocks. Instinctively, he turned away and headed towards the steep route he'd scrambled up two days ago.

As quickly as he dared, he scurried down the slope. It was tough going, as with every step a cascade of dust and pebbles dislodged from under him. The journey wasn't improved by the shuddering reverberations every time Mrs. Bolster threw another boulder.

Relief flooded Finn as, when he finally reached the bottom, he saw Norm, Tomkin and Beth waiting for him.

"Did you get it?" asked Beth.

"Get what?" squinted Norm, not understanding.

"The only thing worth the risk of getting squashed by a flying rock, of course," explained Beth.

Finn didn't answer, but he pulled the shell from his pocket.

"Hooray!!" cried Norm in delight, flinging his pickaxe in the air and catching it impressively. "Hooray for Finn!"

"Alright, alright," said Finn, although he grinned in delight. "We can save the celebrations until we're out of here. Let's go."

Thankfully, the tide was out enough for them to slip and slide their way back over the rocks. No mad giants appeared looking for them, and from the sounds that still echoed from the cliffs, Mrs Bolster was going to be keeping her husband busy for quite a while.

"She is not a woman I want to get on the wrong side of," whistled Norm.

The noises were so loud, Finn noticed several humans were looking at the cloudless sky in confusion.

When they reached the other beach, their parents were packing up their towels.

"Oh good," said Mum when she saw them. "I really don't like the sound of that thunder. It looks clear, but I don't want to be caught out in the rain again."

"We thought we could head into the village for a nice cream tea," said Mrs Barnett. "There are some art galleries too, I've heard?"

Normally, the thought of looking around art galleries with his parents would have made Finn groan with pre-empted boredom. Now, however, he'd do anything to put as much distance as possible between him and the warring giants on the cliff.

"Great idea," he beamed. "Let's go."

After exhausting every delight St Agnes had to offer, the two families parted ways, returning to their cars and cottages. Finn merrily waved goodbye to Bath, promising to meet up soon. Her answering grin told him she understood his unspoken message; they would plan what to do next.

Finn slumped into the car, exhausted but triumphant, Norm and Tomkin both quiet for once.

Finn tossed and turned in his bed, sweat coating his skin as his heart beat faster and faster. In his dream, all was dark. He was in the sea, and no moon shone, but he knew he wasn't alone. Something brushed his leg as he struggled to tread water. Thrashing away, a scream broke his lips. Opening his mouth was a mistake, however, as water flooded in. His scream turned into a gurgle and his head dropped below the surface. Suddenly he could see everything, in that way you sometimes could in dreams. The inky blackness shone with an impossible light, illuminating the creature suspended before him. The morgawr had grown, its massive bulk filling his vision. Its eyes were now red, glowing coals, full of murderous frenzy, and blood dripped from its mouth. A mouth overflowing with knife- sharp fangs.

Then, it lunged.

Finn woke up with a jolt, kicking out so violently Tomkin went flying from the end of the bed. A furious hissing filled the air, and then Norm's drowsy voice joined the fray too.

"What's going on? Is it morning? Why's it so dark? Am I in a mine?"

Finn only realised his rambling questions were muttered in sleep when Norm went on to say, "Oo, a pasty, don't mind if I do."

Loud snoring soon followed.

"What the hell was that?" demanded Tomkin, but in a low voice. He clearly couldn't be bothered to involve Norm.

"Sorry, sorry," whispered Finn, smoothing his duvet to make space for the cat again. "Bad..." he stammered, "Bad dream." The words didn't feel right. What he'd seen didn't feel like a dream, it felt like a premonition.

"Hmm," huffed Tomkin, jumping back up and circling until he was satisfied his spot was well padded enough. "Well, if you could refrain from catapulting me halfway across the room, I'd be most obliged. Otherwise you might find a dead mouse on your pillow when you wake up."

With a final grumble to himself, the cat closed his eyes, and was soon asleep too. Only Finn was left wide-eyed in the darkness. His chest was still pounding, and no amount of deep breaths would rid him of his icy fear. The reality of what he faced crashed into him. Of course, some part of him must have realised where this mission was headed, but when challenged with mermaids and giants he'd somehow squashed down the final terror. All he'd concentrated on was the glory. Now the morgawr was next, however, Finn knew he couldn't do it. Just the thought of seeing it again was enough to make his veins run cold.

As the panic crawled over him, threatening to make him sick, Finn I considered his options. Thinking always helped to calm him, but now every possible scenario he conjured involved the chance of meeting the morgawr. Again and again, those frightful eyes forced themselves into his mind. He stuffed his face into the pillow, willing his brain to offer a solution. At last it complied, but it was not what he'd been hoping for. Giving up was a cowardly choice but, try as he might, no other course presented itself. The knowledge was bitter, yet he swallowed it down, allowing the image of blood-coated teeth to provide the incentive.

It felt wretched at first, almost as sickening as the fear. Then, as his dedication to the decision settled in his bones, his heart slowed its frantic pace. He'd have failed, after everything, but it wouldn't really matter. No one at school would know he'd even tried. He'd simply continue to be the weird, human boy with no friends. As much as that thought stung, it was preferable to the nightmare he'd had. As dawn broke, Finn's fear finally evaporated. His skin was cool and his mind made up.

This adventure was over, and that was that.

He decided not to mention his radical change of heart to Norm and Tomkin. Not yet anyway. After spending all night grappling with himself, he couldn't bear regurgitating all his arguments to convince them. Or convince Norm, at least. Tomkin would no doubt be in full support of his choice to quit. Instead, when he returned from breakfast, he informed them casually that he'd be spending the day with Mum and Dad at a local National Trust garden.

"But we can't plan our next move without Beth," cried Norm.

"I hate to admit it," confirmed Tomkin, "but the gnome is right. That girl does seem to be the brains of this operation."

Not allowing the sting to his pride to show, Finn shrugged.

"They want to cram in a bit more culture before we leave at the weekend," he said.

What he didn't add, was that it had been his idea. That they'd suggested another day on the beach with the Burnett's so he could play with Beth, but he'd refused.

Norm stuck out his bottom lip sulkily, but soon started asking his usual questions about food. Tomkin, though, eyed Finn suspiciously for a moment.

"Shall I get my backpack?" asked Finn.

"No," Tomkin replied slowly. "I think I'll take some time off from chaperoning you. If there'll be no planning, keeping hidden in a garden full of humans is more trouble than it's worth."

Finn released an internal sigh of relief. Norm was

definitely keener than Tomkin to continue the quest, but he was also considerably easier to distract.

It was so bright and warm, Finn was doubly glad to be under green foliage rather than on a shadeless beach. Mum and Dad were happy for him to explore the paths, so he was free to chatter to Norm discretely. It was all rather pleasant, and the weight of the shells and the morgawr lifted from him. The normality of the outing was refreshingly calm for once, rather than frustratingly dull. Unfortunately, Dad then decided to add a bit too much human 'fun' to the proceedings.

They'd laid out a rug in a flower filled field to eat their picnic lunch, Finn managing to keep a whole sandwich to himself for once . He was about to retrieve a book from his bag, when Dad pulled out a bright-red plastic disc.

"I thought we could have a game," he announced to Finn.

"What is that?" asked Finn, immediately suspicious.

"A frisbee," replied Dad, throwing it in the air a few inches and catching it again easily.

Finn's eyebrows rose. His lips parted, all too ready to release a scathing refusal, but the hope in Dad's expression stopped him. The day was going too well for Finn to so readily ruin it. With a silent gulp, he nodded.

"Ok Dad," he said.

Mum got up too, although slightly less enthusiastically than Dad. She'd been quite content lying in the sun, although Finn was very glad she couldn't see how close Norm's bare feet were to her head. Judging by how often she sniffed the air, however, their cheesy smell wasn't invisible. When her turn came, she caught the flying disc easily, a smile growing as she turned towards Finn. He stood a few feet from their picnic blanket, where he'd left Norm dozing. His knees were slightly bent, hands ready. It wasn't until the frisbee was sailing smoothly towards him that he panicked. Flinging both arms in front of his face, he screwed his eyes shut and winced in anticipation. It hit him with a thud, bouncing off and landing delicately on the snoring form of Norm. The knocker had been taking full advantage of the empty blanket, his limbs spread out wide, hat balanced on his over full stomach. Now, he sat up with a start.

"What was that?" he cried, brandishing his pickaxe. When his gaze fell on the offending frisbee, he nudged it suspiciously.

"I'm so sorry, Norm," whispered Finn, hurrying forward. "I'm not very good at catching."

"Why was someone throwing that at you? Are we under attack?"

"No, it's a game," reassured Finn. "Just sit and watch. I won't let it hit you again."

Before Norm could answer, Finn rushed back to Mum and Dad. Gripping the frisbee uncertainly, Finn understood why he'd never played before. How did you even throw this thing? Lobbing it with all his strength, the frisbee somersaulted twice before plonking down a mere metre away from Finn's feet.

"Sorry," Finn apologised to Dad, who strode over to pick it up.

"That's ok," he said. "But try to angle your body sideways a bit."

He demonstrated, and the frisbee flew gracefully to Mum. She, too, talked Finn through what she was doing. This time, Finn didn't cower when she threw, but jumped to one side, letting it land where he'd been standing. Norm appeared at once.

"I want a go!" he declared, eyes bright with enthusiasm.

"No way," hissed Finn. "Sit back down."

"They won't see me," Norm promised. "Their brains will tell them it's you throwing it. Please?"

Finn huffed a sigh.

"Ok," he muttered. "But at least try to make me look good."

"I've got this!"

Norm weighed the frisbee in his hands, training a steely eye on Dad. He flexed and shot the frisbee so fast Finn struggled to follow its trajectory. Until it reached Dad. Evidently expecting little improvement from Finn, he waited with his arms hanging loosely at his sides. He didn't even have time to raise them before the frisbee thwacked into his nose. His scream of pain soared over the grassy field, attracting intrigued stares from passers-by.

"Oops, sorry," said Norm, hopping from foot to foot, wringing his hand apologetically. "I didn't mean…"

Finn didn't listen to the rest, as Mum was leading a howling Dad back to the rug. Blood ran freely down his face, and he cupped his nose with both hands.

"I think it's broken," he moaned.

"I… I …," Finn stammered. "Dad, I'm sorry."

"It's alright love," said Mum. "It was an accident." She helped Dad sit and inspected the damage, using copious amounts of wet wipes until the blood ceased to flow.

Finn waited, pulling on a strand of his hair and biting his lip.

"It's not broken," Mum declared at last. "It will bruise,

but they'll be no permanent damage."

"I'm really sorry," Finn said again. "I'm an idiot." He glared at Norm.

"To be fair," muttered Norm, "he didn't even try to catch it."

"Quite the throwing arm you've got there," Dad said, just the slightest hint of confused suspicion in his tone. "We'll have to get you involved with the local cricket team."

Finn blanched. "I think my sporting days are behind me. I'll stick to reading, much less dangerous," he declared, and before anyone could talk anymore about horrendous team sports he had no intention of playing, Finn pulled out his book and buried his face in its pages.

They left not long after the frisbee incident. The heat from the sun had increased, and Mum declared she needed a swim to cool off. Finn tried to stall, but soon realised he was fighting a losing battle. So he sulked to himself instead, bracing himself for the inevitable.

It was late afternoon when they reached the beach, briefly popping into the holiday cottage to change Dad's blood-spattered top. Despite the time, Finn didn't dare hope Beth's family had left. The beach was crowded, the temperature driving many to the water to find relief. Tomkin, who'd joined them again, sniffed.

"Humans and their water, so odd."

For once Finn agreed with him, although he wasn't looking up to see the source of the splashes he could hear. He was keeping his head down, trying to be invisible, but...

"Finn!"

He shuddered as he recognised the voice. As if he needed confirmation, Norm called back, waving, then yanked on Finn's arm.

"Look, Beth's here."

Finn's jaw clenched, but he stopped. Mum and Dad were already joining Beth's parents, dumping their bags and readying for a swim. Beth, who sat inside a perfect circle of sandcastles, beamed at him.

"I've been waiting all day," she chastised. "I'm so bored!"

"We've had an amazing day," said Norm, and he launched into a re-telling of the dramatic game of frisbee.

Tomkin nestled into the divot of sand next to Beth where she lay her towel out for him. Finn didn't move. Sweat coated his skin, and he cast around to look for any shade. There was none. It was a few moments before they all noticed his stationary form.

"Are you alright?" Beth asked him quizzically.

"Yes," replied Finn, but his tone was icy. He wanted to run away before the inevitable topic was raised.

Beth's brow furrowed, but she appeared to shrug off his weirdness.

"So, did you want to..." she glanced around to check that no one else was listening and lowered her voice, "discuss what we should do now?"

"No," he snapped, laying his towel out as far from her as he could without joining the family along from them. He sat down so hard the fabric bunched in the middle, hot, dusty sand pooling around his bottom. "There nothing to talk about," he growled. "Let's just sit here as long as we have to, trying to avoid getting too much sand in our pants, before we can go home."

"I quite enjoy the feeling of sand in my pants," mused Norm, seemly not fully picking up on Finn's mood. "It tickles."

"Have I done something wrong?" asked Beth, lips parted in shock.

Silence.

"Finn?"

"Are you sure it wasn't him that got hit on the head?" enquired Tomkin, peering at Finn.

"There's nothing wrong with me," retorted Finn. He pulled his sunhat down lower, trying to hide his face. He was sure he could feel tears building up inside him. This was going terribly, but how could he explain? Better to think him horrid than a coward.

"Do… do you not want me involved anymore?" asked Beth quietly. She, too, sounded like she might cry. "If so, that's fine. I won't mind if I'm not magical enough for the next part of the plan."

When Finn glanced at her, he saw her jaw was set, and she even managed a determined smile, despite the liquid swimming in her eyes. Finn crumpled.

"That's not it at all," he admitted. "But there is no next plan. Nothing for you *not* to be a part of. I… I'm giving up."

Fourteen

Fight Or Flight

A stunned silence followed his statement. Finn couldn't look at any of them, and allowed the brim of his hat to hide his blue eyes, brimming with shame. He hunched his shoulders, ready for the onslaught, the accusations of cowardice.

But no one spoke.

When Finn dared glance up, he saw why. Beth had clamped her hands firmly over the mouths of both Tomkin and Norm. For a minute, he was distracted from his torment to register her bravery at placing her fingers so close to Tomkin's teeth.

"It's alright," he blurted, not wanting to be the cause of bloodshed. "You can let them shout at me."

Uncertainly, Beth removed her hands.

"If you must know," growled Tomkin as soon as he could speak, "I was going to rejoice in your sanity, until my power of speech was so rudely violated!"

"I'm sorry," said Beth, "but you two have a habit of talking before you think, and I have a sense Finn is going through something."

"Is that a polite way of saying he's lost his mind?" suggested Norm, apparently unphased by Beth's behaviour.

She ignored him, instead looking at Finn. "Why?" she asked softly.

Finn floundered, wondering if there was any excuse that wouldn't make him seem pathetic. At last he gave up and plumped for the truth. If they were to hate him it may as well be for the right reason. At least being terrified of a sea dragon was pretty rational.

"It's the morgawr," he said, his head dropping again. A lump had formed in his throat, strangling his words so they all came out higher pitched than usual. "I... I can't face it again. I'm too... afraid."

"Of course you're afraid of him," chuckled Norm. "He's utterly terrifying, and he tried to eat you."

"Norm!" exclaimed Beth. "Why would you say that? See, this is why I tried to gag you."

"Something I don't advise you repeat!" Tomkin glared at Beth and swished his tail. "I doubt you'd be as tasty as a mouse, but I don't mind finding out. And why shouldn't we agree with him? He's almost died twice over the last week. That's enough to make anyone reconsider their life choices."

"I'd say it was closer to four," added Norm, counting on his stubby fingers. "But that sounds pretty normal for an adventure. Not that I've been on one before but..."

"Norm, would you like some sweets?" interjected Beth loudly, pulling a packet of brightly coloured jellies from her beach bag.

Norm's green eyes went wide with longing, his wisdom on adventures forgotten.

"Ooo," he practically drooled, accepting the bag and stuffing a whole handful into his mouth at once.

"Finn," said Beth, finally able to talk to him without interruption, "I understand." She drew a deep breath before continuing. "I didn't think I'd be able to face Bolster a second time," she admitted, twisting a strand of hair between her fingers and chewing her bottom lip. "The morning before we went, I almost pretended I was too sick to come. I couldn't make my body move. I remembered the way his hand had felt tightening around me, and I wanted to sink under my duvet and hide forever. I was so, so scared." Her freckled cheeks flushed pink.

"But you seemed so fearless," gasped Finn.

"I was only mirroring back what I saw in you," replied Beth. "And I knew if I didn't tackle the brute, he'd haunt me forever. Now I know I can take on a giant and win!"

"The morgawr isn't the same as Bolster," said Finn. "He... he..."

"Whatever he is, we can handle him together," promised Beth.

Finn saw the certainty in her expression, something he didn't possess an ounce of. But then... did he really want to live in fear of the morgawr forever? Never see an expanse of water without wondering if it lay in wait for him? Still, terror gripped him as he pictured his nightmare again.

"You're not alone," said Beth.

Suddenly, the images in his mind were joined by three more figures. Beth, Tomkin and Norm floated with him, between him and the morgawr. His heart swelled.

Slowly he swallowed, lifting his chin slightly.

"Ok," he managed to say. "I'll try."

Later that afternoon, Finn sat on his bed holding the

two shells in his hands. He was waiting for Beth to arrive and had been contemplating his new decision to finish the mission for some time. As much as the danger continued to eat away at him, when he looked at the shells an excitement swelled in his heart.

"What happens if you put them together?" asked Norm, leaning forward.

Finn had been thinking the exact same thing, but he'd been too nervous to find out.

"I'm not sure," he said. "Do you think it's safe to try?"

"Probably," said Norm, not exactly filling Finn with confidence. "Go on. Give it a go." He then ran across the room and stuffed himself into the wardrobe, peeking out from a crack in the door nervously.

"Ever the hero," drawled Tomkin.

Despite being slightly deterred by Norm's response, Finn took a deep breath and was about to place the two halves together when he was interrupted by a knock at the door. Norm yelped and Finn hastily stuffed the shells under his duvet as Beth bounded in, not waiting for an answer.

"Oh, it's you," Finn sighed in relief.

"What a lovely welcome," she replied.

"Just come in quickly and shut the door, we were about to test the shells."

Beth eagerly hurried in and seated herself in Finn's desk chair, her face alight with anticipation.

"You might want to hide in the wardrobe," Norm advised her, poking his head out momentarily like a meerkat. "They might explode."

Finn rolled his eyes, but then felt serious as he slowly brought the shells close again.

He pressed their cool edges against each other. His fingers tingled, but then… nothing happened. Unsure if he was relieved or disappointed, he pushed harder.

"Nothing," he said unnecessarily. He put the pieces down and they fell apart again, lying innocently. "Maybe you have to be a sea princess for… whatever should happen to happen?" he mused.

"Unless they're the wrong shells and we risked life and limb again and again for nothing?" suggested Tomkin.

"Has anyone ever told you you're not very comforting?" inquired Finn.

"It might have come up," replied Tomkin. "Once or twice."

"I wouldn't worry," said Norm, re-emerging now the danger had passed. "They look like every other shell on the beach, but I'm sure they're very magical."

Finn rubbed his face with his hands.

"Have you got any inspirational words of comfort to add?" he asked Beth, who was frowning at the shells from the chair.

"What are they supposed to do?" she asked.

"No idea," shrugged Finn.

Her frown deepened.

"But, how is the sea princess going to use them? What does she need them for? And how are you going to get them to her?"

Finn scrambled for a reply that didn't make him feel stupid.

"They'll set her free," he said at last, rather lamely.

Beth raised an eyebrow. "You don't have a clue, do you?"

"The riddle's really confusing," complained Finn in defence.

"Let me read it," she demanded.

Finn obligingly handed over the parchment, secretly happy when a look of puzzlement developed on Beth's face.

As she scanned, Norm's voice echoed in his head, a memory of the first time he'd heard the words she was currently reading. Finn let himself listen, the Cornish accent of the knocker lilting in his mind.

I call for the help of a magical child,
One with the strength to take on the wild.
For centuries now, I've been trapped with no power,
An innocent victim, locked in a tower.

The keys to my chains, so tightly bound,
Will not be simply or easily found.
Two shells are required, but not any will do,
These ones are special, for only a few.
Magical blood is needed to see,
To find them and take them and bring them to me.

One forms a lock in the bonds of a creature,
Whose wonderful voice was her very best feature.
With a scaly long tail and luscious blonde mane,
All that have met her remember her name.
In the village of Zennor, she is waiting and plotting,
Whilst all those that wronged her are endlessly rotting.
She hides in plain sight, with my shell as her cage,
A beauty he might be, but beware of her rage.

The second was claimed as a monster's dear prize.
Tread slowly and carefully, for he's a great size.
His temper's quite awful, don't go in for a fight
Defeat him with logic and cunning, not might
Try not to fear, for he's stupid and vain.
Words and quick thinking will scramble his brain.

When both are collected, bring them to me,
Where I shall be waiting, imprisoned at sea.
My Sea Princess power was taken away,
So with no aid from you, I'll be destined to stay.
Take on this challenge, rescue me do.
I'll forever be thankful, indebted to you.

"I'm confused," Beth announced a few moments later, drawing Finn back to reality.

"I told you it's complicated," he crowed. "We've worked out most of it though." He puffed out his chest slightly.

"No," scoffed Beth, "I understand the riddle well enough, but I don't get who this…" she wrinkled her nose, scorn coating her words, "sea princess is? And why you decided to help her?"

"She's not a sea princess," interjected Norm. "There's no such thing as a sea princess."

"That you know of," argued Finn. "And why does it matter if that's her real title or not? She needs help. Does it matter why?"

"Of course it does! All sorts of people might *want* help, it doesn't mean they deserve it. Why was she imprisoned in the first place? And who's holding her captive?"

"The morgawr," replied Finn, although his voice held no conviction.

"But under whose orders? I thought he was just a beast?"

"Er…" Finn started, but he realised he didn't know how to answer all these questions. He looked at Norm and Tomkin, but they had nothing to add.

"And how do you plan to take the shells to her? 'Bring them to me', it's all a bit cryptic, isn't it? How will you find her, if she's locked up?"

"You don't seem to like her very much," said Finn, attempting to change the subject. "Is it because she's a princess?"

"She's not a princess," whispered Norm.

Not that anyone listened to him.

"So," said Beth, cocking her head to the side. "You ran off and undertook a life-threatening quest without knowing the answer to *any* of these questions?"

"She needs our help," Finn repeated pathetically. "What would you have done?"

"Oh, the same," admitted Beth fairly, "but I might have thought a tiny bit about who I was helping and, more importantly, the enemy I could encounter."

Finn winced. "Do you really believe there's something worse than the morgawr out there?" He couldn't imagine anything more terrible than the creature that made he want to curl into a ball and give up again. He shivered.

Beth shrugged. "Even if there isn't, do you seriously expect there won't be an obstacle to stop you getting to her? You can't simply chuck the shells in the ocean and hope she finds them!"

All Finn's previous doubts pushed themselves upon him again. He slumped under the weight of them, despair biting at him. His new resolve to fight to the end was drifting away.

"Why are you being so negative?" he huffed. "Earlier you wouldn't stop nagging me not to give up and now… I was right all along," he wailed, throwing his arms up, "we should forget the whole thing ever happened."

"No, no, no," cried Beth, jumping to her feet. "We are *not* giving up. That's not what I'm saying at all. I just want us to be prepared."

Finn nodded, but the worry had already wormed its way back into his gut.

"Finn," Beth insisted, leaning on the bed and looking up at him "We can do this, but we have to be smart about it."

Finn nodded again. "Ok. What did you have in mind?"

"Firstly," said Beth, straightening, a gleam of excitement appearing in her hazel eyes, "we need to get our hands on a boat."

Finn spluttered. Even Norm's jaw fell slack with shock, and Tomkin snorted.

"Is it too late to take her back to the giant?" Finn said to Norm.

"We should probably scope out one with easy access in the daytime tomorrow, so we don't have to waste time looking in the dark," Beth continued, seemingly unaware of the horror she'd produced in her audience.

"Have you gone completely and utterly insane?" Finn cried. "Or have you always been this bonkers?"

"You shouldn't be unkind," said Norm gently. "She had quite an ordeal with that giant. And he *was* waving her around quite a bit the other day. Maybe he shook her brain a bit loose?" Norm peered at Beth in concern. "She does look a little wonky," he added in a not-so-quiet whisper.

"Oi," cried Beth. "I do not look wonky! I expected rudeness from the cat, but not *you* Norm."

"I wasn't planning to involve myself," sniffed Tomkin, "but as you're content to drag *my* name through the mud, I have to agree, you *are* acting a little crazy."

"Have any of you got a better idea?" Beth challenged.

"Yes, actually," said Finn.

"Really?" Beth raised an eyebrow in disbelief. "What?"

"Well, I know you were joking before, but if I tie the shells to the bottle the riddle came in, and put it in the sea…"

"I knew it," crowed Beth, interrupting him. "You've got nothing!"

"That's a reasonable plan! For all we know, that bottle's got some sort of tracing magic on it and it'll lead her straight to it."

"Uh huh, sounds likely," scoffed Beth.

"Why are you suddenly so keen to deliver the shells directly to her? Before, you seemed to think she was tricking us, and now you can't bear the thought of her not getting them?"

"I just feel that if you're going to do something, do it properly."

"And..." pushed Finn.

"And... I don't know, I want to see her."

Finn paused as Beth sighed.

"And," she admitted after a moment, "I don't want all this to be over so quickly. It's been... amazing. Like a story from a book."

"There's still Norm and Tomkin," reassured Finn. "They're all weird and magical. You can spend as much time with them as you like. And," Finn lowered his voice, "you can take one of them home with you if you want."

Norm gasped in affronted shock.

"I'm joking," said Finn, although he grinned at Beth. "Anyway, you two are being suspiciously quiet for once. What should we do? Risk our lives or assume 'bring them to me' means place them in the sea?"

"Er..." Norm looked from Finn to Beth, "I'd rather not say. I don't want to pick sides."

"I love arguments," said Tomkin, "but, in this case, you're both wrong, as neither of you are suggesting we abandon the stupid quest and lie in the sun."

"You two are both massive disappointments," said Finn.

His words caused Tomkin to bow in satisfaction and

Norm to look sadder than Finn had ever seen him. A silence filled the air as the stalemate hung between them all. Beth fixed him with a steely stare.

"What about the morgawr?" said Finn. "And the insignificant fact he's got a taste for my blood, and if I go anywhere near the sea he'll probably appear and eat me?" He felt rather dramatic, but the fear of that beast still kept him awake at night.

"We could rub you in seaweed?" suggested Norm. "To disguise your... smell?"

"I think I liked it better when you refused to get involved."

"Come on," cajoled Beth. "Don't you want to end this adventure properly?"

Finn groaned, but he knew he'd already lost.

"Fine," he cried in defeat. "Let's creep out of bed in the middle of the night, steal a boat and set out into the ocean in search of a sea princess but avoiding the morgawr who wants to devour me."

"Hooray!" beamed Beth, jumping up and down in delight.

"This couldn't possibly go wrong at all," muttered Tomkin.

Fifteen

Boating For Beginners

The conversation about where they could acquire a boat was far from simple. The fact the water around Falmouth was littered with vessels did little to make it any easier.

"Maybe we could borrow one?" Beth had suggested.

"Not without an adult's help," Finn had replied. "And I don't know about your parents, but there's no way mine would let me sail off into the ocean all alone."

"Hmm, you're right," said Beth, nodding. "We'll have to temporarily steal one."

Despite his many issues with Beth's plan, Finn agreed to go out and look. They all split up to scan the surrounding area. Finn's search was half-hearted at best, and he was happy to head back to his cottage after an hour with no possibilities. The others, he saw, were already gathered, and Beth looked far too triumphant for his liking.

"I've found one!" she declared, confirming his fears.

"Seriously?" he said. "You've found a boat we can easily 'borrow' and take to the sea in the middle of the night without getting caught?"

"Yep. Well," she conceded after a pause. "A sort of boat, anyway."

"I warn you," said Finn, "if you're referring to body boards, I may well have a tantrum."

"His tantrums are quite impressive," teased Norm. "You should say it's body boards just for fun!"

Finn scowled at him, and the knocker backed off, holding his hands up in surrender.

"There is nothing fun about body boards," said Tomkin.

"What have you found?" asked Finn resignedly.

"It's a canoe," announced Beth. "And, the best bit is that it comes with my holiday cottage, so we won't even have to steal it!"

Whilst Finn had to admit that the idea of avoiding theft was appealing, the notion of a canoe was *not*. He'd never actually been in one before, but everything he'd seen told him they were even less stable than the boat he'd had to endure with Mum and Dad.

His face must have clearly transmitted his emotions, for Beth's smile dropped.

"Did *you* find anything?" she challenged, placing her hands on her hips.

"No," he replied.

"Then a canoe it is," she said.

"Hooray!" cried Norm, before tilting his head to one side. "What's a canoe?"

Finn half hoped that he'd get caught. That he wouldn't succeed in creeping down the stairs as the clock struck midnight, taking each step one at a time in case they creaked. To his amazement, however, he was outside breathing in the cool, summer night air before he knew it.

"Good to know how easy that was," said Norm.

"Why?" asked Finn.

"For the future."

"No. This is it. After I've finished with all this madness, I'm done with adventures. If I ever find a message in a bottle again, I'm going to put it in the bin without even looking at it."

"Finally, you speak sense," cheered Tomkin, but Norm only placed his finger to his lips and whispered, "Shh!" loudly whilst surveying the empty street.

Finn stuck out his tongue, but stayed silent as they made their way towards Beth's cottage. It was only one street over, and they were there within minutes.

"She's there," said Tomkin, his cat eyes seeing far more in the dark than Finn could.

Not wanting to be outdone, Norm reached up to flick on his head torch.

"Don't," hissed Finn. "Not until we're away from the houses."

Finn had a torch too, but it was safely enclosed within the bag slung across his back, along with the bottle, note and both pieces of shell. He'd felt he should pack more, like rope or other such survival objects, but he couldn't find anything remotely useful in the cottage. Anyway, the bag was heavy enough as it was.

"You made it," whispered Beth in relief when they reached her. "My heart is pounding so fast, this is crazy."

"It's your idea, remember?"

"Are you going to remind me of that all night?"

"Only when things go wrong," replied Finn.

"The canoe's in here," she said, pointing to a small, ramshackle shed in the front garden.

Finn followed her as she carefully unbolted the door and swung it open, cringing as it creaked slightly. Hurriedly, they lifted an end each and carried it out onto the street. It wasn't heavy, but so cumbersome it made walking awkward.

"The coast is clear," said Norm, taking on the role of lookout. "Let's go."

Finn glanced up at the surrounding houses, but no lights had been flicked on whilst they'd been moving the canoe. Thankful for that at least, he followed Norm towards the beach.

As he stood on the shoreline, the waves lapping unnervingly close to his feet, Finn started to have second thoughts. The liquid was as black as ink, and a chill breeze ruffled his hair. It wasn't the cold air that caused him to shiver, though. It was fear. Spine tingling terror at what might be hiding beneath the surface.

"I can't," he said, in barely more than a whisper.

The others all stopped.

"Can I just try and throw it back in first? Please?" He knew he sounded pathetic, but he didn't care. Before they could list a hundred reasons why his idea was awful, he yanked the bottle and shells out of his bag. He didn't know how to attach them together, however.

"Here, use this," said Beth, pulling a hair band from her hair. One of her reddish-brown plaits unravelled, so she pulled at the other one too, stowing that band on her wrist.

"Don't you think I'm being an idiot?" he asked in confusion.

"Yeah, but it can't hurt to try. And then I can always say 'I told you so' as we get in the canoe!"

Finn knew she was humouring him, but took the hair band anyway. He wrapped it around the shells, securing them as best as he could to the bottle's neck. Then, he tentatively placed the whole thing into the water. It bobbed gently, floating in front of him. They all watched and waited. A minute passed, then another.

"Sea Princess?" Finn called as loudly as he dared.

Tomkin snorted, but at least Norm didn't tell him they weren't real again.

Nothing happened.

"Are we going to watch it all night?" yawned Tomkin. "Because, if so, I might have a nap."

"No, it's fine," sighed Finn, reaching down to scoop the bottle up again. As his fingers passed through the surface of the water, a strange sensation tingled up his arm. Everything went too quiet, and he could have sworn a ripple spread out to sea. Glancing at the others, they didn't seem to have noticed anything.

"Let's get this over with," he said, shaking himself mentally as he wiped his hand dry on his shorts.

Thankfully, the waves were calm and small. Finn didn't like to consider how they'd have managed if it had been rough. As it was, it was tricky enough to simply climb *into* the canoe without tipping it over.

Tomkin jumped in on dry land and refused to do anything other than sit in the very centre and shudder. Norm was barely more help.

"Careful," Finn hissed again and again, and he was more than a little wet by the time they were all seated.

"Where first?" Beth asked, picking up one paddle and handing him the other. "Straight out, or along the shoreline?"

This had been the point in Beth's plan where an element of 'winging it" had been settled upon. None of them could decipher a location hidden in the riddle, however much Beth tried. Therefore, they'd decided to see what drew them, hoping Finn's magical senses would kick in. They all looked at him expectantly now, but Finn couldn't feel anything other than a shivering fear. The vastness of the ocean felt overwhelming, especially when he thought of what it contained.

"Let's not go out too deep," he said at last. "Maybe along the coast? Close to land?"

"So close I could jump to it and watch from there?" suggested Tomkin.

Ignoring the cat, Finn and Beth started to paddle.

"Whoopie!" cried Norm. "Canoes are fun!" Then, a couple of minutes later, once Finn and Beth had rotated the vessel in a perfect circle no less than three times, he clutched the side dramatically. "I think I'm gonna to be sick!"

"You and me both," said Tomkin. "You know, I believe the theory with these things is that you go in a straight line!"

"It's not that easy," snapped Finn. Even Beth was looking a flustered. She opened her mouth to say something but froze. Finn stared at her before realising her gaze was fixed on something behind him. Something out to sea. Dread filling the pit of his stomach, he turned. He didn't need to guess what he'd see. He knew in his bones.

A row of spines glided towards them, protruding impressively and glinting like knives. A shadow beneath the surface, darker than the water itself, entirely encircled the canoe. Finn was suddenly back in his dream, every muscle tensed, his eyes frantically scanning. The head, when it finally burst upwards, reared until its red eyes found Finn. It stared only at him, ignoring everyone else. Beside him, Beth clapped her hands to her mouth in horror. Norm yelped and dived beneath his seat, and Tomkin growled, low and deep. Finn, froze, hypnotised by sight before him, his living nightmare.

If possible, the morgawr was even more terrible upon second viewing. Up close, Finn could see the scales that overlapped in perfect precision, iridescent in the moonlight. Wetness dripped off its horns, which twisted savagely upwards, ending in a lethal point. Around one, a pure band of gold shone, so strange it snagged Finn's attention for a second, the whirls and patterns branded into it stirring some memory. Then the morgawr opened its mouth, and his focus was one hundred percent on the rows of jagged teeth. They had no blood on them, but they dripped with saliva, a promise of violence to come. The rotten stench of fish washed over him.

Finn braced himself, knowing he should move, run, do *something*, but could not convince his limbs to budge. Slowly, that maw stretched wider, but rather than attack, it simply let out a putrid huff of breath.

Finn winced, and a shudder ran down his body. Then the creature retreated, sinking back beneath the waves. Finn didn't relax. This was not over, he felt sure. A moment later his fears were confirmed. The canoe moved, and not of its own accord.

"He's pulling us," said Norm, peering over the edge.

Sure enough, the morgawr's tail was wrapped around their tiny vessel, dragging them forward.

"Are you alright?" asked Beth. It was then Finn realised he was still locked in place. He was clutching the sides of the canoe so tightly his knuckles had turned white. His breathing was fast and rasping, and he suspected he was having some sort of panic attack.

"What's it doing?" he squeaked. "Why didn't it try to eat me? Where's it taking us?"

"To our impending doom, no doubt," said Tomkin.

"You're not helping." Beth shot him a warning glare.

"I wasn't trying to," Tomkin snapped back. "Why would I try to help when all my advice is so regularly ignored?"

"Don't mind him," said Norm. "He's just cranky being so close to water."

"Yeah, it's just the water," sneered Tomkin. "Not the sea dragon that's dragging us off to his lair to eat us, one by one."

Finn squeaked.

"You don't know that," reprimanded Beth.

"Don't I?" replied Tomkin. "Then what's that up ahead if it's *not* a lair?"

His words had them all staring ahead. The light on Norm's hat faintly illuminated the cliffs before them. One patch, nestled in deep, was darker than the rest; a cave.

They were headed straight for it. Finn could feel the panic rising in him like bile.

"We've got to do something," he said, but before he could say more, they were thrust forward. The morgawr flicked them, sending the canoe bumping over the waves, and they plunged into the pit of darkness. At last they stopped, the canoe wobbling unsettlingly. Finn glanced behind them, and could make out the beast's body, wedging into the entrance of the cave, forming a wall of scaly flesh. They were trapped.

"See Tomkin, you were wrong," echoed Norm's voice from beside Finn. "He's not devouring us. He's merely trapping us in the dark."

"Maybe he's not hungry," replied Tomkin. "Or maybe he's delivering us to his master."

"Will you give it a rest?" snapped Beth.

Finn, however, asked, "What do you mean?"

"It's like Beth mentioned before. Do we really believe that the morgawr is the mastermind behind capturing this princess? Or is he working for someone else? Has the overgrown snake just added us to the cage?"

Finn gulped. "But then, if this is the cage, shouldn't she be here?" he said, glancing around, not that he could see anything in the gloom. "If we can give her the shells, she can escape and get us out too."

"Who says that's part of the deal?" said Tomkin. "I wouldn't hand over those shells until you've got a promise of help if I were you."

"I hate to agree with the world's most pessimistic cat, but he's got a point," said Beth.

Finn subconsciously slipped his hand into his pocket to check the shells were still safely hidden inside. He wished his brain would start working. He knew if he could *think* he'd be able to make more sense of this whole mess, but the appearance of the morgawr had rendered him practically dumb. The most he could do was study their surroundings. Somewhere above, a slither of moonlight shone. There must be a small opening up there, but it did little to penetrate the blackness in front of him. It certainly didn't let Finn fathom how big the cave was, or how far back it went. He could hear water gently lapping against rock, and the drip, drip, drip of moisture everywhere. It did nothing to ease the tension.

They all fell silent; blind, waiting.

Just when Finn thought he might explode with anxiety, a new light appeared. Initially, he thought his eyes were playing tricks on him. Green, glowing splodges danced across his vision, causing him to blink rapidly. Only when it grew did he notice it was coming from beneath the surface. It rose, spreading until it illuminated the entire cave. Finn glanced at his friends, their expressions a range of terror, awe and mistrust that he was sure must mirror his own. All of them held their breath as they waited.

A moment later, the source of the light appeared.

Sixteen

The Sea Princess

When a face emerged, Finn had nothing left in him to be shocked. Ghost-like, the figure of a woman flowed upwards, stopping to shimmer just above the surface of the water. Her head and torso were entirely transparent, but it was easy to see her beauty. Long hair twisted around her shoulders, and she wore a gown that somehow looked regal despite having strands of seaweed trailing from it. There was no crown on her head, but Finn suddenly felt that Norm had been wrong; *this* was a sea princess.

Finn knew he should be elated. Before him floated the person they'd been seeking, the one he'd imagined himself describing to the kids at school. And yet, trepidation coursed through him, chilling his veins.

The sea princess rolled her head on her neck, stretching, and took a deep breath.

"It has been so long since I tasted air," she said, more to herself than any of them, her voice strangely rough, as if unused for a long time.

A second breath had her smiling, softly closing her eyes to revel in the moment. When she opened them again, they fixed instantly on Finn.

"You have them," she said. It wasn't a question.

"Was it you that asked for our help?" It felt like a stupid question, but Finn didn't want to hand the shells over to just anyone, not after everything they'd been through to get them.

The princess nodded.

"I so infrequently had the strength to reach out. Even when I did, there were never any wizards to help. When my morgawr smelt your blood, however, we both knew the chance had come. That salvation was in reach."

"It... it was helping you?" Finn asked in disbelief. "Then why did he try to eat me?"

It was a petty thing to focus on, but he couldn't simply accept the morgawr was actually good!

"Morgawr's have strong instincts," she said, glancing at the beast, something strange in her expression. The morgawr lifted its head to look at her, and Finn could sense emotions he couldn't fathom being passed between them. It didn't improve his nervousness.

"I can only apologise for his actions," the princess went on, "and thank you for agreeing to aid me, anyway. I was beginning to think no one ever would."

"If the morgawr didn't capture you, then who did?" asked Finn, earning himself a nod of approval from Beth. If there was another danger lurking, he wanted to know about it.

The woman's face went stony in an instant, and Finn half wished he hadn't raised the point.

"I will not speak his name," she said. "Suffice to say, he no longer dwells in this realm."

"Why did he imprison you in the first place?" Beth's voice was high and reedy, a clear indication of her terror.

The sea princess shot her a quick glance, but returned her full attention to Finn when she answered.

"Rude," Finn heard Beth mutter under her breath, but very, very quietly.

"*He*," the sea princess said, almost spitting out the word, "was my enemy for many years, and I his. We fought countless times, but our final battle was brutal. He tried to kill me, and most thought he had, but he could not. I'd put in place countless spells throughout my life to prevent such a thing. However, having defeated me, he would not let me go. His power was also very great. I was stripped of my mortal body and entombed in the water, submerged and trapped in this very cave for centuries. I couldn't access my magic and had no way of seeking help."

"What changed?" interjected Norm. It was the first time he'd spoken since the princess had arrived, and Finn didn't think he'd been around the knocker for so long without hearing him talk before. Norm was standing close to Tomkin, a hand on his pickaxe handle, and they were both staring at the sea princess with mingled fear and distrust on their faces.

"As time passed," the princess answered, still only to Finn, "the world changed. The old magic faded, and with it so did my bonds. But not enough. I can still not set foot on land, can still possess only this glamour of a body. And I can't even stray from this coastline. I thought I was doomed to wait for centuries more until I heard of something that gave me hope; the shells."

They all waited for her to go on.

"It was an old sea god who told me of them, Carraba,

wizened and faded from memory now too. He had long since lost one, and sold the other, but he said that, if combined, they could grant a powerful wish. A wish that could even give me back my body and return me to my former glory. I became obsessed, searching for any clue that might tell me where these two shells could be. I tasked any who would to find them for me. Unfortunately, I discovered they were on land, the hardest place for me to access. That was when the wait for the help of a wizard started. It has been decades, my dear boy, but here you are at last. Please, let me see my prize?"

Finn didn't understand why, but every instinct inside him was shouting to keep the shells hidden. He gave himself a mental shake and forced his hand to move and pull them from his pocket. He held his arm out, over the edge of the canoe, but kept his fingers tightly closed.

"I can't make them work," he said. "Maybe they're not the right ones?"

Beth gave him a sideways look, and Finn knew he was being odd.

The princess ignored his words and reached out, her palm flat. Finn reluctantly opened his fist and dropped the shells into her hand, trying to swallow the lump that had formed in his throat. Tomkin brushed against his legs, a silent rumble passing from his chest into Finn's skin.

"As with so many magical objects," said the princess, staring in awe at her prize, "they require a particular something extra to reach their full potential. In this case, it's the second reason I needed a wizard."

Tomkin growled, audibly this time, and Finn could see Norm calmly withdraw his pickaxe from his belt.

"What do you mean?" asked Finn, trying not to allow himself to become overwhelmed by the rising sense of danger in the air.

"Blood, my dear boy," she said with a reluctant sigh. "Magical blood is such a powerful thing. As mine no longer runs in my veins, I must look elsewhere. I am sure you can oblige."

"No!" cried Beth.

"Er…" stammered Finn.

"I only need a drop," continued the princess serenely. "Or two," she added with a smile that did nothing to reassure.

Time stood still as the princess' request hung before them.

One part of Finn's brain told him to get on with it. That once it was done they could all go home and never attempt an adventure again. But another stayed his hand, advising caution. He was stuck, only vaguely aware of his friends whispering to each other next to him, presumably wondering why he'd lost his ability to function.

"Who are you?" he asked at last, hoping to ease the worry in his veins.

"No one you'd know, I'm sure," she replied. "Now please, I don't appreciate being kept waiting."

The threat in her voice was clear, and it made Finn jerk back instinctively, which was not the best thing to do in a canoe. The vessel wobbled, banging into a rock he hadn't realised they were so close to. It wasn't a hard enough knock to damage the boat, but caused Beth to fall forward in front of him. To add to the confusion, Norm suddenly jumped onto the rock.

"Quick," he shouted as he yanked at Finn to follow him.

It was then Finn realised that Beth hadn't fallen, but stooped to pick up Tomkin. She, too, was now leaping for the rock, the cat ludicrously large in her arms.

Not understanding at all, Finn scrabbled after them, allowing Norm to pull him up by his t-shirt. He only just managed to find his footing. The rock was so slippery with seaweed, jutting out of the sea like a mini island in the middle of the cave.

The princess let out a tinkling laugh. "You believe you're safe there?"

"You said you cannot set foot on land," shouted Norm, positioning himself in front of Finn defensively.

"But I have developed my restricted powers enough to control the waves in this cove."

Finn didn't ask what she meant, not as the water level instantly began to rise. He'd gawped, transfixed, fear making his skin clammy. He didn't know what to do. Didn't know how to save his friends. Not without his magic. The way they encircled him, putting themselves between him and the woman he no longer thought was a real princess, made him feel even more helpless. Desperate to help, he scanned the cave. The canoe was still bobbing invitingly, but with the morgawr wedged in the entrance and the waves becoming ever wilder, he knew that was a fool's choice. The walls, what he could see of them in the gloom, were slick and wet, offering no ledges to clamber up. Above, however, the distant hole in the roof twinkled enticingly. The night sky it revealed resembled salvation, albeit an impossible one. They had no way of reaching it.

"I'm on it," shouted Norm, who'd been monitoring Finn's gaze.

He pulled a rope out from the inside of his filthy jacket and wrapped it around himself. "A good miner goes nowhere without a rope," he declared.

In an instant, he'd slung it over his shoulder and fired himself at the cave wall with a leap Finn didn't think was possible. He climbed so fast he resembled a four-legged spider. How he gripped the slick stone, Finn couldn't fathom. In a matter of seconds, he'd reached the hole at the top and vanished through it.

Finn only had a moment to glance at the princess, to check she was too focused on channelling her power into the waves to have noticed Norm's departure, before the knocker's face re-appeared. Silently, he dropped down the rope.

"Go," hissed Beth from beside him.

Finn didn't need to be told twice. Pulling once on the rope to test its strength, he launched himself up onto it, and shimmied. Or at least, attempted to shimmy. Rope climbing was evidently far harder than he'd imagined. Unfortunately, to add to the situation, his flailing attempt had drawn the attention of the princess. She turned slowly towards them, death in her eyes. Finn struggled harder, finally getting high enough to make room for Beth, who had Tomkin draped around her shoulders. The sea water was now lapping over the rock they'd been standing on and, as the princess narrowed her eyes at them, it churned violently. Panic overwhelmed Finn. There was no way he'd be able to climb faster than those waves.

Suddenly, with an almighty cry of "Hold on to your pasties!", Finn felt himself flying upwards. Norm, face red with the effort, was pulling them. They swung alarmingly, banging painfully into the sides of the cave, but then they were at the hole. Finn scrabbled, knees scrapping on stone and nails digging into the earth as he put everything he had into clawing out onto the cliff.

At last he was out, and he flopped down onto damp grass, panting as he stared up at the night sky. Rolling over, he saw Beth slumped on her side, breathing deeply. Tomkin, back arched, was hissing at the hole, and Norm was bent double, coated in sweet. Finn thought they might have stayed like that for hours, shock and relief rendering them immobile, but a scream of frustration had them all on their feet in a flash. Water jettisoned out of the hole, spraying them all, then the cry of anger shifted into a braying, cruel laugh, tinged with madness.

"You think you can escape me?" the princess' voice crooned up to them. "Just holding the shells has started to magnify my withered powers. The waves sing to me, begging to do my bidding. Soon, so soon, it'll be fully mine to control. This bay of humans won't have time to scream for mercy as they drown, as their houses are submerged. When dawn breaks, I will unleash myself upon them. I will ensure all remember the name Morgan Le Fay and rue the day they left me to rot."

Her cackle trembled the earth beneath Finn's feet.

"Only you, dear boy, can save them," she continued, her tone now soft and caressing, seeming almost to whisper in Finn's ear. "Only you. Come to me before dawn. Give me your blood, and I will spare the humans and their town. I swear it, on everything I hold dear. The choice is yours."

Finn paused, the weight of her words lying heavy upon his soul. Then Beth was grabbing his wrist, pulling him forward. Beside them, Tomkin was leaping. To Finn's amazement, Norm straddled the cat's back, hands tightly clutching fur to stop himself slipping off.

None of them looked behind. They just ran. Ran away from the sea, away from the cave, back inland, to the illusion of safety.

Seventeen

A Brief History Of Evil

It was a risk, all of them entering Finn's cottage, but they needed the comfort of four walls around them. Thankfully, his parents were heavy sleepers, and he didn't hear them stir as they tiptoed down the hallway and closed his bedroom door softly behind them.

"What do we do, what do we do?" repeated Norm over and over.

"Shh," said Finn, trying to remain calm. He knew no humans could hear Norm, but his own brain needed quiet to think.

"Who is she?" he asked after a moment. "Who is

Morgan Le Fey?"

He looked expectantly from Norm to Tomkin, who were surveying each other.

"You tell them," said Tomkin, uncharacteristically serious.

Norm opened and closed his mouth like a goldfish, but no words came out.

"Is it that bad?" asked Finn.

"Worse," said Norm. "Worse than worse."

"Just start at the beginning and tell us everything," instructed Beth calmly.

"It all happened so long ago. Way before my time," said Norm, "but the magical folk of Cornwall will never forget the stories surrounding Arthur, not when so many of them took place on our very soil."

"You don't mean *King* Arthur, do you?" asked Finn. "With the knights? And the round table?"

"That's the one," confirmed Norm. "He and his followers did great things in their day, but they also faced troubles. Troubles like Morgan Le Fey. She was born here, you know. Her father was an honerable lord at Tintagel, but evil grew in her veins. She hated Arthur, her half-brother, allowed to rule as she never would be.

"Not sure I can blame her there," interjected Beth.

"History wasn't kind to girls."

"True," shrugged Norm, "but she turned to dark magic in her attempts to seize power for herself. Thankfully, Arthur had Merlin to protect him."

"You're not telling me he's real too?!" interrupted Finn.

"Merlin was the father of all wizards," informed Norm. "When he departed our world, he left behind his magic to be shared by a few. It's how the race of wizards started. You've read about that in one of your books, surely?"

Norm was correct, Finn had, but it was merely a theory. One of the many theories about how the wizarding race had formed, each as unsubstantiated as the next. Finn had never really *believed* any of them.

"He was a great friend to Arthur," Norm continued to explain, "and he saved him at the end. When Arthur and Morgan battled for the last time, Merlin stepped in. He was too late to prevent the fatal blow, but he kept Arthur alive long enough to take him to Avalon."

"What happened to Morgan then?"

"The stories all say that Merlin killed her," said Norm.

"Evidently, the *stories* are all wrong," said Tomkin.

"Well, yes, about that bit, I'm guessing they are," conceded Norm. "But the bit about her existing isn't."

"Obviously," said Tomkin dryly.

"This is all well and good," said Finn, "but is there anything in all these stories that might help us now? Some lovely little weakness we can take advantage of? A combination of words that will re-trap her in that cave and stop her killing all the inhabitants of Falmouth, maybe?"

"Er... no... sorry," said Norm. "Mostly they detail how evil and unstoppable she is."

"Great!" grumbled Finn.

"So, she's powerful, and she's got the shells, and once she has a drop of magical blood she'll have her body back and probably start reeking terrible revenge?" summed up Beth.

"Remind me never to let you read me a bedtime story," said Finn.

"What, you see a silver lining in all this, do you?"

"No, but... well, surely it's not all as bleak as that?" He looked hopefully at Norm, who'd always been able to put a positive spin on things until now.

"It's probably worse," the knocker cried in defeat, throwing himself face first onto Finn's pillow and howling loudly. His fists clutched the fabric, which only mildly muffled the sound, and his jacket rose to reveal a glimpse of his disturbingly hairy back.

Dejected, Finn collapsed down next to him and placed his head in his hands.

"There's no point moping about it," said Beth. "And there's even less point making that noise," she added as Norm's wails went up a pitch. "We need to come up with a plan. Finn, why can't you use your magic? Surely you won't get into trouble if you save so many lives?"

"It's not that I haven't been willing to use my magic all this time," explained Finn in exasperation. "I literally *can't*. They bind it before I leave for the school holidays. There's no way I can create a spark." Speaking the words made him feel depressingly useless.

"What about one of your teachers? Or *any* grown up wizard? Can't you contact one of them to come?"

"There isn't time. Wizards don't have mobile phones. A message could take days to reach anyone. We barely have hours."

He glanced at his watch. 2 o'clock. Dawn would be around 4. Could they even evacuate all the humans before then? That's assuming anyone believed him for a second, which he seriously doubted. As these helpless thoughts whirled around inside his mind, he withdrew from the conversation. He was only partly aware that the others continued to brainstorm, Beth firing a myriad of questions at Norm and Tomkin. Time ticked ominously on, and eventually silence filled the bedroom as all ideas sputtered into nothing. No one addressed the question of what they'd do if they couldn't think of anything.

"We have to return," declared Finn suddenly. The words surprised him slightly but, as he said them, he knew it was the right thing to do. "I have to stop her. I just have to."

"You're not going to give her your blood, are you?" gasped Beth. "That won't help anything in the long run."

"No," said Finn. "I'm going to get the shells back and use the wish myself."

The confidence Finn was trying to present was slightly dented as Norm fainted to the floor in shock. Colour drained from his usually rosy cheeks, and even his beard looked limp.

"Norm!" he and Beth cried, shaking him gently until he stirred.

"Drama queen," muttered Tomkin, not moving an inch to help.

"Sorry, sorry," said Norm, sitting up slowly. "Tonight has been rather a lot already." He picked up his hat from where it had fallen off and placed it determinedly on his head. "But I am ready to support you, whatever you choose to do. Even if that's…" he gulped, "returning to face that witch."

"Thanks Norm," said Finn, feeling quite emotional at

212

the support. "And I do have a plan," he went on, looking at Beth and Tomkin.

"I'll reserve my declaration until after I've heard it," said Tomkin.

Beth said nothing, but she watched him, arms folded, waiting. With her hair no longer restrained in plaits, it spilled around her face wildly, yet did nothing to soften the intensity of her gaze.

"Ok," started Finn, hoping his idea sounded as good as it did out loud as it did in his head. "We go back, pretending we want to give her some blood. I'll use the hole in the top of the cave, and stay attached to a rope so I can get out if anything goes wrong. Then, when I reach out to let my blood drop, we'll use a distraction so I can grab the shells and make my wish instead."

The stony silence response told Finn he hadn't done a very good job of convincing them.

"What would distract her that much?" asked Beth, her tone kind but definitely uncertain.

"I was thinking the morgawr?"

"What? The ferocious beast under Morgan's control that almost certainly wants to eat you?" asked Tomkin. "That morgawr?"

"Yes, but I've got a theory about him," explained Finn.

213

"Norm, didn't you say that morgawrs are usually peaceful creatures who live off krill and small fish?"

"Yes," said Norm, "but, there must be exceptions. There's no doubt he's helping her."

"Yes, but what if it's not out of choice?"

"Stop being cryptic and explain what you mean," ordered Tomkin.

"I am," insisted Finn. "When he was close to me, on the canoe, I noticed it had this ring of metal around one of its horns. It didn't look natural. It had all these strange markings on it too. Then, when we were in the cave, the way Morgan and it looked at each other. It was like he *hated* her. I think she's controlling him against his will, through that ring, and if we remove it, he'll be on our side."

"Wow," said Tomkin. "Did you hit your head on the way out of that cave?"

"I know it sounds far-fetched…"

"Crazy," corrected Tomkin.

"*But*," Finn went on forcefully, "I'm certain. I have that magical intuition, or whatever it's called."

"I don't know Finn, it feels like a big gamble," said Beth. "I'm not saying we *shouldn't* go, but maybe we should have another distraction up our sleeves, just in case?"

"Fine, Tomkin can launch himself at Morgan and claw

her eyes out, whatever you want," said Finn. "It doesn't matter, I *know* I'm right."

"Excuse me, but I haven't actually said I'm coming," said Tomkin.

"Oh, come on," cajoled Norm. "Surely you owe me again? I'm pretty sure I saved your life again earlier."

"Why else do you think I permitted you onto my back?" cried Tomkin. "The lumps of fur I'm currently missing definitely paid off that debt."

He turned in an exaggerated circle on the bed, and Finn noticed that his usually immaculate fur was matted and dishevelled in places.

"It was an impressive rescue, though," said Finn.

Beth nodded in agreement.

"Fine," sighed Tomkin, scowling at them all. "Why not risk death one more time? I only have nine lives after all!"

"Thanks Tomkin," said Finn. "It would be wonderful if you could. I have a feeling Beth and Norm are going to need all the support they can get freeing the morgawr and convincing it to help us."

Eighteen

Wizards And Wishes

They didn't continue to discuss the details of the plan after mapping out the basics. Time, as Finn kept pointing out, was not on their side.

Before long, they were creeping back out of the cottage, Tomkin grumbling to himself. The night felt more dangerous as they headed for the cliff path. No one spoke much. They all knew their roles, and no words would add any certainty to what was about to happen. When they reached the spot, Finn waited as Norm looped a collection of ropes around a large boulder. He didn't ask why Norm kept so many ropes at hand; he was simply grateful that he did.

Once Norm was satisfied that the knots were all secure, he turned to Finn and began wrapping another around his waist. Next, he did the same to Beth.

"You're to climb down this one," he said, handing her a different rope, "but you'll also be attached to the top of the cliff. If you fall, it won't be pleasant, but you shouldn't crash to your death."

"Reassuring," said Beth, her brown eyes wide and panicked in the moonlight.

"Same goes for you," said Norm to Finn. "Although, without the safety rope, you'd probably just break a few limbs. It's a much less dangerous fall."

"Lucky me," replied Finn.

Beth managed to chuckle, although the sound was too high pitched to fully hide her terror.

"What about you?" Finn asked Norm.

"I don't need a rope to climb," Norm laughed before he walked over to the cliff edge. "Beth, follow me, and try not to dislodge too many rocks, this hard hat can only take so much."

Then he was gone, clambering so fast Finn could barely spot him when he leaned over to watch. He could hear the waves crashing below, hidden in the darkness, but there was no sign of the morgawr. Finn could only hope he was there, ready to be befriended.

Gulping, Beth picked up Tomkin and wrapped him around her shoulders again. She gave her rope a nervous pull before she dropped to her knees and, very clumsily, backed off the cliff. She said nothing but, when she looked up at Finn, he saw a steely determination in them.

"Good luck," he mouthed as she went.

Tomkin only hissed in reply.

Seconds later, Finn was alone. Now he had to wait. Not for long, just enough for them to reach the bottom. Then he would go to face Morgan. Make sure all her attention was on him whilst his friends attempted to entice the morgawr. Beth carried a bag of fish from his fridge that they all hoped would do the trick. However, just in case, Norm carried a screwed-up tissue soaked with a drop of Finn's blood. Finn *really* hoped that it wouldn't be necessary.

Once he was certain enough time had passed, Finn stepped up to the hole they'd escaped from earlier. The water level had thankfully receded, and the green glow that softly reflected off the dank walls reassured him Morgan was still in her cave. Gritting his teeth, he sat, dangling his legs inside the hole. Fear enveloped him as he dropped down the rope, but he knew the others would already be approaching the morgawr. If he didn't move, Morgan might see them. Closing his eyes and hoping Norm was as good at tying knots as he was at climbing, he pushed forwards.

He slid, faster than he'd expected, the skin of his hands burning in complaint. Miraculously landing on the rock, which barely poked above the water now, Finn didn't release the rope as he scanned the cave. His sight struggled to adjust, but Morgan's glowing figure was hard to miss. She faced him regally, a smile dancing on her lips. Her back, thankfully, was towards the entrance, and Finn didn't dare attempt to look for his friends. He didn't want to risk arousing the witch's suspicion.

Instead, he squared his shoulders and met Morgan's gaze.

"My dear boy," she crooned. "How pleased I am that you could re-join me. You left in quite a rush before. In fact," she leant towards him, "some would have called it rude."

She was teasing him, triumphant in her win. Finn struggled to find the words to respond. The little canoe bobbed beside her, remarkably undamaged. Finn noted it, adding it to his list of possible escape routes.

"I don't advise a water escape," said Morgan, noting where his attention flickered and correctly guessing his thoughts. "Anyway, I have no desire to cause you harm. You and your friends have helped me. Where are they, by the way?"

Her pupils narrowed.

Finn kept his face neutral. "They wouldn't come with me," he said. "They think that helping you will make things worse."

"And what do you think?"

"That I can't let hundreds of people drown because of me. I hope that if I help you, then your retaliation will be directed at someone who's actually wronged you, and not innocent people."

"You're a sweet thing," said Morgan, neither confirming nor denying his statement. "You remind me of my brother, before that evil wizard got to him and turned his head with power." Anger rippled off her as she spoke of Merlin. Finn kept very still, not wanting to do anything to direct that anger upon himself.

"Anyway," she said, with a roll of her shoulders, letting go of her tension. "Let's get started, shall we?"

She held out the shells in one hand and, more alarmingly, a small silver blade in the other. "Don't worry, it'll only hurt for a moment."

Finn hesitated, wishing he knew how the others were getting on. Should he stall further, or were they now waiting for him? It was impossible to tell. He hoped the fact the morgawr hadn't reappeared was a good sign but...

"What will you do?" he asked, deciding to delay a tiny bit longer. "When you have your body and powers back?"

Morgan surveyed him thoughtfully, as if debating how much she should reveal.

"I am afraid your hopes for me are far too generous," she said, a sad smirk playing on her lips. "I don't care that *he* is long gone from this realm. I despise him and all his stock. I am glad you didn't force me to kill humans tonight. Not because I care, but because I want the first ones I kill, once I am restored to my former glory, to be those descended from him."

"What, his family?"

"You're all his family, don't you understand?"

Morgan laughed at Finn's slowness at following what she was saying.

"All.

Of.

You."

Finn gasped, comprehending at last. "Wizards?" he whispered. "You hate all wizards?"

"Hate is not strong enough a word," Morgan spat. "Wizards are an embodiment of *him*. They all contain his blood, however diluted. I will kill you all."

"You can't," said Finn, shaking his head numbly.

"But I will."

"You can't blame us for what he did to you? And… and…" he added lamely, "you said you wouldn't hurt *me*!"

"Actually," corrected Morgan, "I said I had no desire to. The reality is, I must. But not yet. There are hundreds to make suffer before it'll come to that. You may have the honour of being the last of your kind to die, if you want? And your friends are not wizards, so they'll be free to go."

Despite her reassuring tone, Finn didn't feel in the least bit better.

"Now, hold out your hand," she commanded.

Finn took a deep breath, stealing himself for what he was about to attempt. Or at least, what he hoped he was about to attempt. If the others didn't appear, then his only choice was to try to wrestle the shells from Morgan by force. Disregarding the fact she was far more powerful than him, he wasn't even sure he could touch her transparent body. Maybe he'd simply fall through her and splash into the sea.

Pushing aside his doubts, Finn slowly held out his arm, palm upraised. Morgan approached with the knife. The cut didn't hurt, was no more than a nick, but it had blood welling within a second. He resisted the instinct to pull it to his lips, to stem the flow. Instead, he kept his arm ridged as she brought the shells close. Her pale hand dropped the knife, its job done, and slid around his wrist. Finn shuddered at the touch. Her grip was firm, but with the coolness of wet, dead fish. She looked him square in the eyes, wicked glee twisting her pale features, as she moved the shell towards his dripping blood. She'd clearly waited a long time for this moment and was savouring every second.

Now, Finn thought, desperately trying to send a message to the others.

But no one appeared, no beast rallied to their aid. Finn braced himself to jump at Morgan, knees bending slightly.

Just a little closer… a little closer…

The shells lay invitingly on Morgan's palm, shining with their own light. Grabbing them wouldn't be the challenge, it would be fighting off her hold. He rose on the balls of his feet, ready… Then, the most amazing sound filled the air. It was so deafening that, in the confines of the small cave, it was almost unbearable. A moment later, the source of the roar appeared, and Finn couldn't help the cry of joy that ripped from him.

The morgawr filled the entrance, eyes burning with hatred, its gaze locked on Morgan Le Fey. She stared back in shock, but didn't let go of Finn's wrist. Just then, three other faces appeared on top of the sea dragon where they sat riding him as if he were nothing more than a friendly horse. Beth, Norm and a surprisingly enthusiastic Tomkin were all grinning as they added their triumphant roars to those of the morgawr. Morgan's fingers lost their tension, and Finn burst into action.

Yanking himself free, he grabbed at the shells with his blood free hand. They slipped from Morgan's outstretch palm, his fist clamping around them so tightly he feared he'd crush them to dust. Stumbling backwards, Finn had no time for triumph. Morgan turned from the morgawr and snarled with a fury that chilled his veins.

"Give them back," she hissed.

Her hatred hit him like a physical force.

"I've changed my mind," she growled at him. "You have earned the honour of my first kill after all."

Finn's brain was screaming at him to get the hell out of there, but his feet wouldn't move. He was frozen to the spot. A movement to his right caught his eye. The morgawr was charging, diving right for Morgan, but with a wave of her hand the water churned and rose, forming a solid wall. The morgawr and Finn's friends were on the other side, and Finn was trapped. The dawn light was shut out too, and the cave was suddenly much darker. Morgan's green glow was pulsing, a visible representation of her anger, a spiky and dangerous thing.

"Give. Them. Back."

Finn struggled to think. Then, the rest of his plan came slamming back to him. As quick as he could, he clasped his hands together, coating the shells in his blood. They were slippery, and he worried he'd never get them to attach, but as soon as the edges met they fused, a pure white light shining from the seams, filling Finn with hope.

"Don't!" Morgan cried, but Finn blocked her out as he opened his mouth to shout his wish.

But he paused.

Temptation filled him momentarily. Thoughts of greatness, being bathed in glory for his knowledge and power. Finn knew he could wish for all these things. Be as powerful as Merlin had been. Grant himself such magic that the school could never bind it again. Then he could re-imprison Morgan with no help. Trap her so tightly she could never bother him again.

However, an image of the mermaid of Zennor popped into his mind. Her misery because of the retaliation of others. He knew he couldn't inflict such pain, no matter how deserving the victim. His thoughts cleared, and he spoke.

"I wish that you, Morgan Le Fey, were good. That you

were free of your prison, but could never turn to evil again."

He said the words carefully, just as he'd planned them with Beth. They'd written out a multitude of different combinations, for once encouraging Tomkin to point out every flaw he could find. If there was a loop-hole, it was one none of them could think of, yet Finn was nervous.

The world went still.

Morgan's mouth opened in a soundless scream.

Then, everything happened at once.

Nineteen

So Good It Hurts

Light, bright and blinding, forced Finn to screw his eyes shut. Peeking through his lids, he could just make out the wall of water as it came crashing down. It rushed around his legs, and he clung to the rope for dear life. He swayed precariously until eventually the churning sea calmed and he scrabbled onto the rock. With the wall gone, he could glimpse the morgawr, filling the cave entrance, his friends still perched on its back. Shielding his eyes, Finn desperately scanned the cave for Morgan. When he saw her, horror filled his mouth like bile. She floated, suspended completely above the water, the source of the light holding her in place.

As Finn watched, her greenish tinge faded, and a pinkness flowed over her skin. Black hair materialised, framing her calm face, youthful and empty of hate. Her eyelids flickered, as if she were dreaming, but remained closed as the transformation continued down her body, altering all of her until, as suddenly as it had arrived, the light vanished. The magic complete, Morgan fell. She dropped with a soft splash, causing barely a ripple. The surface closed over her head, swallowing her whole. Colours flickered in Finn's vision as he struggled to see where she'd gone, but the dimness had returned to the cave and all he could make out was a stream of bubbles. They each popped, one by one, and silence stretched as he realised she wouldn't re-emerge. Not on her own.

Sliding off his rock, he plunged in without giving it a second thought.

It was shockingly cold, yet he barely noticed as he thrashed his limbs, surprised at how deep it was. The floor of the cave was unreachable, and his pathetic doggy paddle was doing little to keep him afloat. Regardless, he reached forward, searching for Morgan with his hands. He couldn't be responsible for her death, even if she was evil. He couldn't stand by and allow her to drown. At last, fabric brushed against his fingers and he clutched on tight, just as his own head dipped beneath the surface. He didn't have the breath to call for help. Salty water rushed down his throat and his eardrums filled with the sound of muffled shouts. Too late, he remembered the others. That they had been far better suited to attempt a rescue mission. As despair clawed at him, cold scales pushed themselves against his torso, propelling him upwards. He clung onto what he hoped was Morgan.

Cool morning air caressed Finn's face, coaxing his lids open. He was met with the terrifying sight of the morgawr's eyes. Bolting upright, he realised he was straddling the beast's tail, dripping wet but safe. Next to him, sprawled and still unconscious, the body of Morgan lay on her back. Her skin was pale, hair plastered across her forehead, but Finn could see her chest rising and falling, ever so slightly.

"Well that was dramatic," called Norm, popping up between the morgawr's horns. "Perfect for when you retell this story. Proper hero stuff!"

"Thanks Norm," said Finn, his voice hoarse, speaking an effort.

"Get her in the canoe," said Beth, appearing next to Norm.

Finn didn't have the energy to ask how on earth he was supposed to do that when the very act of holding his own head up was making him faint. Thankfully, the morgawr lowered its tail and gently tipped Morgan, and then him, into the canoe. It rocked worryingly, but steadied quickly as the morgawr held it against his body, preventing any seawater from spilling in.

"Let's get back to shore," Finn heard Beth say. "Dawn's on the way."

Finn watched as the morgawr, with its three triumphant passengers on top, pushed the canoe with its snout out of the cave. It then secured it in the crook of its tail and swam smoothly towards land.

As if in a dream, Finn reached his hand out, daring to touch the arc of scales that hugged the canoe, marvelling at their softness and iridescent colours. He avoided looking at the limp body of Morgan, curled in the hull. It was enough to know she was alive and breathing. The reality of what the ancient witch had become, and all because of his wish, was something he couldn't deal with at that moment.

The journey back was a bit of a blur for Finn. Dawn broke as they approached the sandy shore, staining the sky with a mix of pinks and oranges. The beach was empty, but logic told Finn it wouldn't remain that way for long. Nor would his parents' ignorance as to his disappearance. However, he couldn't make himself hurry as he helped Beth lift Morgan from the boat and lay her on the sand.

The others all gathered around, staring down at her suspiciously.

She lay so motionless she could have been dead. Black hair fanned out, swirled in patterns as if she were still floating through the sea. It was long, past her waist in places, and shone like midnight. Her skin was translucent, like the uncooked flesh of fish. Her newly formed veins were visible in places, snaking in blue rivers up her neck. Her limbs jutted from the scraps of blue dress that hung on her. Finn felt he could snap her bones merely by looking at them too hard.

"Is she really alive?"

"Is it even her?"

"She looks... different?"

"What if it's some kind of trick?"

Questions bombarded Finn, but he didn't take his attention from the unconscious figure.

"It's her," was all he could reply.

Tentatively, Finn reached down and gave her a little shake. She moaned, almost inaudibly, and frowned, although her lids remained clamped shut.

"Maybe a sharp kick would help?" suggested Tomkin. "I'm pretty sure she deserves it after everything she's put us through, however 'good' she might be now."

The morgawr, who loomed above them, seemed to snort in approval of Tomkin's suggestion. Beth, however, tutted at them both.

"Let's give her a chance, shall we?" she said.

Norm, who'd climbed rather reluctantly off the morgawr at last, strode forward.

"Wake up," he ordered in a surprisingly forceful tone for the usually chirpy knocker. "Otherwise we might let the morgawr decide what to do with you, and he exclusively informed me he's more than happy to change his preferred diet of fish. Just this once."

"Norm!" chastised Beth.

"This youthful appearance doesn't mean the innocence has spread inside," replied Norm seriously. "Be careful," he warned.

Finn understood what Norm was saying. Even though he'd chosen his words carefully, the wish *may* have gone awry. But he'd felt the power of the shells course through him. It had to have done more than simply change Morgan's appearance? Surely?

Summoning all the confidence he could muster, Finn put all the force he possessed into his voice as he called out, "Morgan Le Fey, wake up."

At last, the lifeless figure opened her eyes. And screamed.

The sound was terrible. It burnt at Finn's flesh with its intensity. A release of pure pain and fury. Her pupils dilated, and her newly pink flesh drained white.

"What's happening?" cried Finn, although he doubted the others knew any more than he did.

Indeed, Beth shared his expression of horror, Tomkin was backing away, and Norm hopped from foot to foot, hands clamped over his overlarge ears. Only the morgawr remained unmoving, watching Morgan with an expression of satisfaction. He, after all, had suffered most at her hands. Almost as quickly as it had started, the scream stopped, cut off as if by magic. Morgan's mouth clamped shut, and she sat upright in a single lurch, pinning Finn with a piercing glare.

"What have you done?" she demanded, the venom in her tone at odds with the girlish voice that came out of her. "What am I?"

"I... I don't know, exactly," admitted Finn. "Human? Or a wizard?"

Norm sniffed at her. "She's not human?" he declared. "But not quite a wizard either. There's magic in her blood, but... it's different."

"It's not my blood I care about," growled Morgan. "What have you done to my..." she clutched her arms around herself. "Heart? Soul? Feelings? I have such strong *feelings*, and none of them are very familiar."

"What do you mean?" asked Finn.

"I feel… I feel…" Morgan closed her eyes as a ripple of agony passed across her features. "I feel so much. And it hurts. Remorse. And guilt. For what I did. What I was. It's… overwhelming."

"And what about Merlin?" asked Finn tentatively. "And your plans for revenge?"

"Merlin?" murmured Morgan, as if the name felt foreign on her tongue. "I remember everything that happened. Our years of conflict, but I feel… indifferent!" She paused, brow furrowed. "And when I try to invoke the rage I should have," she went on through gritted teeth, clutching her sides again. "Pain. Horrendous pain and regret. How is this possible?"

Finn stepped away as Morgan scowled and continued muttering to herself.

"What do you think?" he whispered to Beth, Norm and Tomkin.

"She could be acting," mused Norm, "but if so, it's quite convincing."

"I don't trust her," announced Beth. "She seems pretty angry for someone you wished to be good."

"Good people can be angry," said Tomkin. "I'm *very*

good but perpetually annoyed at so many things."

"You're not good," laughed Norm. "You torture mice for pleasure."

"Ok," conceded Tomkin, "I'm mostly good. Still, my point remains. She's permitted to have feelings, even negative ones. The question is whether or not she can act on them, or if she's now got the conscience to stop her turning to evil."

They all turned to watch her again. A deep scowl dented her otherwise smooth face. As Finn studied her, he realised that she was now probably about the same age as him. Like the wish had returned her to an age that would allow her a second chance at life. She was wringing her hands together, wincing every now and again. Then, slowly, a small ball of orange light built in her palms. Magic. She definitely had magic, and it was strong too. Finn gulped as he took in the flames. He knew what it could do to them. How he'd be powerless to protect them if Morgan decided to push it out towards them.

"Every time I think about punishing you all for what you've done," she said, "I get this awful jerk of... moralistic horror. So strong it hurts!"

She clapped, and the light disappeared.

"I look at that thing," she cried, gesturing towards the morgawr, "and feel the urge to apologise! This is awful!"

Relief washed over Finn, and he let out a long breath. "It worked," he sighed.

"Yeah, but she's not exactly *nice,* is she?" said Norm. "I don't think many magical creatures will rush to claim her."

Morgan stuck her tongue out at them.

"I understand you're going through some sort of emotional breakdown after your personality transformation," said Tomkin, "but could we put it on hold?"

"Yeah," agreed Finn, "we should get off the beach before anyone arrives."

He glanced at their bedraggled group. Even if the morgawr and Norm were invisible, they made an unusual sight. He was sure that any adult would be annoyingly interested in the half-drowned girl lying on the sand. And that was a complication they could certainly do without.

"Let's go," he ordered.

"You can leave me here," said Morgan. "I can look after myself."

"Not a chance, princess," said Norm. "You come with us."

"Fine," she huffed, clearly realising that a battle wouldn't be worth the effort.

They waited as she got to her feet and, as they turned, it occurred to Finn that the morgawr couldn't come with them.

Emotions swirled as his past fear struggled to withdraw. Swallowing, he stepped towards it, refusing to let himself shake.

"I can't thank you enough," he said solemnly.

The morgawr lowered his head and pushed its nose into Finn's belly. He stifled his scream as it huffed out hot air, which wrapped around him, ruffling his hair. He laughed.

"You're not scary at all, are you?" he said. "You're borderline cute!"

"We'll come and visit tomorrow," promised Norm, rushing forward to embrace the dragon's neck.

Tomkin walked forward, but rather than deliver the sarcastic comment Finn had expected, he bowed politely.

"Thank you for the ride, Seaweed," he said. "It was a pleasure."

Finn shared a surprised look with Beth.

"Seaweed?" he asked, unable to keep a straight face.

"I named him," said Tomkin, his glare daring Finn to challenge him.

"Of course," said Finn, biting the insides of his cheeks.

"Let's go," called Morgan, breaking up the emotional goodbye. "Otherwise I literally might cry, and I really don't want to."

Her eyebrows were so tightly knitted together, Finn

could only imagine the internal turmoil she was going through.

Then they made their way back. Their luck held, and they met no one all the way to Finn's cottage. The second he pushed open the front door, however, Finn knew it had finally run out.

"Finnley Jacobs," cried Mum. "Where on earth have you been?"

Twenty

The End Or The Beginning

"You're wet," Mum exclaimed as her eyes raked over Finn. "Again. Why are you always wet at the moment? And Beth? You're involved in all this? I thought you were... normal?"

"Oh, I am," Beth attempted to reassure her, an impossible task under the circumstances.

"And who's this?" she pointed at Morgan as Dad appeared behind her.

Finn opened and closed his mouth, trying to think of any explanation that wouldn't make this situation worse.

None presented themselves.

"Shall I remove the glamour on me and Tomkin?" asked Norm. "Then we could help explain?"

"No!" cried Finn in alarm, before realising shouting to apparently no one was definitely not the route to take.

"Mum, Dad, things have been a little... unusual here in Cornwall," he said. "I've faced a few magical trials, like homework, that I wasn't expecting."

"This is to do with school?" asked Dad.

"Um... yes," said Finn, deciding to go with it. However much his parents feared magic, they still believed strongly in the education system, even if his was slightly different.

"Then why didn't you tell us?" he asked.

"I know how uncomfortable you are with all things magic," reasoned Finn. "And I didn't want to ruin your holiday."

Mum and Dad shared a sad, guilty look, and Finn knew he'd convinced them.

"And these two?" asked Mum.

"Beth is just someone I met here and wanted to help," explained Finn. "As she said, she's completely normal and human. And Morgan is..." he faltered before pushing on, "from school. We didn't expect to meet here."

"Oh, ok," said Mum, eyeing Morgan more suspiciously than before, as if having it confirmed she was a wizard made her more unappealing. "Are you staying close by?"

Morgan raised her eyebrows in question to Finn before he stepped in to answer for her.

"Yeah, a house around the bay."

"And are your parents aware you've been out all night, doing whatever's made you soaked through?"

Morgan let out a snort of laughter. "My parents are dead, but even when they were alive they couldn't have cared less what I did."

A stunned silence followed Morgan's words.

"I'm so sorry, dear," said Mum softly, surveying Morgan with sympathy now.

"I'm not. And if I was, a thousand years is a long time to heal."

"Oh, this is priceless," said Tomkin.

Finn forced himself to laugh. "Morgan's got quite the sense of humour," he said. "Anyway Mum, we're sort of in the middle of a project that we need to write up. We need to send it off to school this morning, so… can we go?"

Mum pursed her lips and Dad rubbed his temples as if he were getting the start of a headache.

"Fine, fine," they said.

"But please, change into something dry. And lend your… *friend* some clothes too," pleaded Mum as Finn started towards the stairs, "otherwise you'll get ill."

Finn agreed as cheerily as he could before herding Morgan up to his bedroom.

Once he'd shut the door, very firmly, he leant back against it, exhaustion overtaking him.

"I hate lying," he groaned.

"On the plus side," said Tomkin, "you're getting better at it. That was almost believable."

"Thanks."

"Do you always do what those humans tell you?" asked Morgan. "As a wizard, you outrank them, you know."

"They're my parents and I'm ten. Being human or wizard doesn't have much to do with it."

"Hmm, curious," she muttered. "This being mortal thing is going to take some getting used to. Especially being a child. Do you know how long it's been since I was a *child*?"

"What are you going to do with her?" Beth whispered to Finn as Morgan continued to rant.

Finn exhaled loudly in response. "I need food before I consider that impossible question," he replied.

"Did someone say food?" piped up Norm. "It feels an unreasonably long time since I last ate. How many meals have we missed?"

"It's not even five in the morning yet," said Finn.

"Usually you'd still be snoring your head off. You haven't missed a thing."

"Hmm, I'll take your word for it, although my stomach tells me otherwise."

"I'll get what I can," agreed Finn, as *his* stomach more than agreed with Norm for once. "Keep an eye on *her*."

Norm uncooked his pickaxe at once and crouched in place, as if ready to pounce at a moment's notice.

"Change first," instructed Beth. "If your parents are anything like mine, they'll have a fit if they see you're still wet."

Finn couldn't disagree, and he grabbed a handful of dry clothes to change in the bathroom on his way. He also found a clean outfit to offer Morgan. She frowned sceptically at the shorts and t-shirt, inspecting them as if they might come to life and eat her, but he left Beth to explain the modern fashion and slipped out into the hallway. His parents were downstairs nursing large mugs of coffee when he entered the kitchen, and he smiled jovially at them as he explained he and his friends were rather hungry. It was proof of their discomfort at the presence of Morgan that they didn't insist he and the girls come and eat at the table, but allowed him to pile up a tray with what he hoped was enough food to share around *and* feed Norm.

"Breakfast," he announced when he returned to his room. Morgan had thankfully changed, but the human clothes did nothing to detract from her strangeness. Although her hair was now brown, and her skin retained none of its former greenness, she still radiated something otherworldly. She didn't hold herself like a child, and her eyes... Finn couldn't look at them for too long. They swirled with power, with what she truly was. They made him hope that the wish he'd cast was strong enough to contain her. If the true Morgan Le Fey ever escaped her new body, he didn't want to guess what she'd do to him.

"FOOD!" cried Norm, bringing Finn back into the moment.

"Who other than Norm is hungry?" he asked. "Morgan?"

She sniffed suspiciously at the tray Finn carried, but nodded. "Yes, insanely so," she admitted. "Is that normal?"

"It depends," said Finn. "If you're an irritating knocker, then yes. Otherwise, it could have something to do with your body being new. Who knows?"

Finn decided not to ask if she'd needed to eat in her previous form. He didn't want to know what she'd consumed.

After they'd all eaten, Norm predictably gobbling down the lions' share, they all sat around the room awkwardly. The comfortable companionship they'd developed over the past few days was shattered by Morgan's presence. She didn't say much, but watched them so intently when they spoke that it was impossible to forget she was there. There also remained the problem of what, exactly, to do with her. It loomed over Finn until he felt its pressure so strongly he had to address it.

"You'll have to come home with me," he declared after a bout of awkward silence. "We'll tell my parents your aunt needed to leave in an emergency, but she asked if you could travel back to London with us tomorrow, and then to school on Monday. It's only three days."

Even as he said the words, Finn knew it wouldn't be how his parents would see the situation at all. He could already picture their pursed lips and disapproving frowns, but he had no choice.

"Why can't I just go off on my own?" grumbled Morgan. "I'm over a thousand years old, I don't need looking after."

"NO!" snapped Finn. "You're not going anywhere until I hand you over to my teachers."

"It's nothing personal," added Norm, leaning forward and patting her arm gently. "But you were a raving lunatic who planned to kill the entire wizarding race. We're not sure we can trust you."

Morgan huffed in frustration. "Fine. But what will happen to me then? If you think I'm going to let anyone lock me away again, you're sorely mistaken. I don't care how 'good' I am, I'll fight to protect myself."

"No one will hurt you," promised Finn, and he hoped against hope this was true. "But I don't know what to do with you long term. I'm a child too, remember."

Morgan rolled her eyes, but she thankfully dropped the subject of fighting.

"So, you'll all leave together tomorrow?" asked Beth. "That's... nice. I go home then too." She smiled, but sadness radiated from her.

Awkwardness filled the air, broken only when Norm started to cry. Not gentle crying, either, but great guttural sobs, accompanied by streaming snot.

"Why don't you take that one with you, so you're not lonely?" suggestion Morgan.

"I've already tried that," said Finn. "Apparently he's mine, and there's nothing I can do about it."

"I bet you could if you really tried," said Morgan, squinting at Norm. Then, a second later, she threw her arms up in disgust. "Eurgh, no, just the thought of hurting him makes me sad! This is awful."

They all laughed then, breaking the tension.

"You can come and visit," Finn insisted, turning his attention back to Beth. "Well, maybe not at school, but during the holidays? And I'll write. All the time."

"I should hope so. You have to keep me up to date with how *this*," she gestured at Morgan, "turns out."

Finn snorted a laugh. "One thing's for sure," he said. "No one's going to think my *human* holiday was boring this year."

"Can I suggest that now is not the moment for goodbyes," said Tomkin, "but one for sleep?"

Finn laughed, but a yawn came out.

"For once," said Norm, launching himself onto the bed and causing Tomkin to bounce in the air, "I must concede the cat has an excellent point."

Without any more talk, Finn gathered blankets and pillows and spread them out on the floor. They all settled down, Morgan taking the entire bed for herself.

Soon, the only sound to be heard was the gentle rumble of Norm's snores.

Printed in Great Britain
by Amazon